A DIFFERENT MAN

Visit us at www.boldstrokesbooks.com

A DIFFERENT MAN

by

Andrew L. Huerta

2021

A DIFFERENT MAN

ISBN 13: 978-1-63555-977-4

Warning: The author warns all readers that this work includes stories about gay men. If anyone has any objections to homosexuality or reading about the lives of gay men, the author suggests that you seek out other works of fiction.

A Kiss Between Altar Boys first appeared in *Creating Iris*, http://www.creatingiris.org/magazine and *Queerly Loving*, https://queer-pack.com/
Good Help first appeared in *Jonathan*, http://siblingrivalrypress.com/jonathan/
Sex, Love, and Intellectual Property first appeared in *Chelsea Station Magazine*, http://chelseastation.typepad.com/chelsea_station/
Superman's Forest first appeared in *The Round Up Writer's Zine: The Pride Edition*, https://www.roundupzine.com/archives
Paul and Cézanne first appeared in *Hashtag Queer, Volume 2*, https://qommunicatepublishing.com/product/hashtag-queer-lgbtq-creative-anthology-volume-2/

THIS TRADE PAPERBACK ORIGINAL IS PUBLISHED BY
BOLD STROKES BOOKS, INC.
P.O. BOX 249
VALLEY FALLS, NY 12185

FIRST EDITION: SEPTEMBER 2021

CREDITS
EDITORS: JERRY L. WHEELER AND STACIA SEAMAN
PRODUCTION DESIGN: STACIA SEAMAN
COVER DESIGN BY JEANINE HENNING

Acknowledgments

I want to thank my husband, Daniel C. Davis, for his enduring support, and my colleagues at the University of Arizona for their friendship and encouragement.

To my mother, Nancy S. Huerta,
who taught me to appreciate my difference.

CONTENTS

BLESSINGS IN CHILDHOOD

Amelia's Crying

The Potomac River is about two miles from our house in Arlington, Virginia. I grew up in that house, and one day when I was seven years old, Papi, my sister Amelia, and I walked to the river during the shad run. After the waters of the Potomac begin to warm up in the spring, American shad can be easily spotted as they swim inland to spawn. Knowing this and having it marked on his 1974 *Virginia is for Lovers* calendar, Papi brought home a large fishing net. He told me and Amelia that we were going down to the Potomac to catch enough shad to feed the entire family all summer. He also told us we didn't have a choice. We had to go with him.

So, after a cold and quiet walk to the banks of the Potomac, Papi and I prepared for our fishing. Amelia, who was fifteen at the time, wandered off and sat on a tall, flat rock. She stared out over the Potomac and watched as thousands of shad ran through the river. Their bluish-green backs would pop up in the water and reflect brightly in the sun. There was no denying that the river was overflowing with them, more than enough to feed our entire family all summer.

"Pablo!" Papi yelled. "Pay attention. Next year, I'll buy you your own net, and we'll fish together." He stood on a group of rocks next to the water, holding a long wooden pole with a stringed fishing net at one end. It looked like a butterfly net made of thick, white string woven together to make a large pouch to catch the fish. Papi moved himself into position, held the net out over the water, and stood perfectly still.

"Come here!" he yelled. "Stand next to me and watch."

Papi and I stood together on the rocks just over a small hollow. The water below was shaded and the fish would swim into the opening to rest. As I stared down, dozens of fish sat perfectly still below us as if they were waiting for Papi to reach down and scoop them up with the net. Some fish swam in and out, but more and more gathered beneath Papi's reflection. With a quick breath, Papi plunged the net into the water and pulled up a bunch of fish. He groaned as he held the net out in front of him. Six or seven light gray fish with black and bluish-green backs filled the net. He threw the fish behind him, and they smacked loudly against a large rock on the riverbank. Once they hit the ground, the fish wiggled around in the dirt like a bunch of Mexican jumping beans.

"Here, Pablo," he said. He stepped off the rocks and grabbed one of the fish. "We gotta kill 'em now." He held the fish by its tail and smashed its head against the large rock. When he threw the fish back down on the ground, it didn't wiggle around anymore. One after the other, he hit the fish against the rock, and when he was done, he handed me the net. I took it and stared at the yellow and red spot that was left on the large rock. All of the fish lay still on the ground, and Papi walked over and brought back our ice chest.

"Go!" he yelled. "Go use the net. We need more fish, so go! I showed you how to do it. Now it's your turn."

I took Papi's place on the rocks and stared down into the water. The hollow began to fill with fish again, and all I had to do was get the net down there and scoop them up. As I stepped forward, the wooden pole slipped from my hands, and the net dropped down into the water. The white string of the net ballooned out like a parachute in front of me. All the fish darted away before I could regain my grip on the pole. I was never going to be able to move as quickly as Papi.

"No, *pendejo!*" Papi moved onto the rocks and stood behind me. He leaned against my back, placed his hands over mine, and pressed down hard on the pole. He made me swing the net back out of the water, and we waited for the ripples to go away. When the water was still, only one small fish remained in the alcove.

"There, Pablo! A small fish for a small boy. Get it!" Again, the net dropped into the water and his hands squeezed mine tightly. He pushed the net out in front of me and together we scooped up the small fish. It wiggled around as I held the wooden pole out in front of me. Papi let go of my hands, pointed over at the large rock, and stepped away from me. I flung the net toward the rock, but the pole slipped through my hands. It flew forward and landed in the sand just in front of us. Thankfully my small fish was still in the net. Papi rolled his eyes. He pulled my fish out and dropped it down in front of him.

"It's your fish." He held the pole at his side and walked back toward the alcove. "Kill it and put it in the cooler with the others." He patted my back, but it was more like pushing me forward. I stood over the fish, looking at Amelia. She stared at me but quickly turned away. When Papi was over the water, standing perfectly still with the net poised to strike, I picked the fish up by the tail. I held the thing at arm's length in front of me. It didn't smell, and it wasn't slimy at all. But I just couldn't smash its little head in. I kicked the rock with the bottom of my sneaker. Papi never looked back, so I threw my wiggling fish into the cooler and slammed the lid shut. I turned and ran to Amelia.

"Pablo!" Papi yelled. "Come here and help me!"

I sat down on the rock next to my sister. Together we watched Papi take more fish out of the water and throw them over by the large rock. He held the pole out over the water again and stared back at us.

"I don't wanna fish!" I yelled back.

"Amelia!" Papi yelled. "Come help me!"

She just stared at him. She squinted her eyes and tightened her lips. "No, I don't think so!" she said, staring out over the water again.

"*Pinche jovenes,*" I heard Papi say.

As Amelia stared forward, Papi returned to his fishing. He pulled more and more fish out of the water and threw them over by the large rock. But now he didn't leave his perch and smash their heads in. He just left the fish lying on the sand and returned to his work. I was glad. Amelia held her left hand down at her side, first looking at me and then over at Papi. When Papi thrust his net down into the water, she brought a half-smoked cigarette to her mouth and took a heavy puff.

"Ay, Amelia," I said. Papi was still busy with the net, and Amelia blew her smoke into my face. "Stop it!" I yelled, waving the smoke away. Papi turned and looked at us. Amelia continued to stare at the water, and I turned and looked over the Potomac, too. The water flowed quickly in front of us, and I noticed other people fishing on the opposite side. They worked with large fishing nets like we were, pulling dozens of fish out of the water. Papi said when we got home, he would teach me how to clean the fish and prepare them for cooking. I exhaled heavily, as I was not looking forward to that.

❖

Papi set up two banquet tables in the backyard and piled all of our day's catch on one of them. I stood a short distance away and watched to see if any of the fish would move. But they didn't. Their eyes stared at nothing and their little mouths hung half open. I walked around the table looking for my small fish. Most of the shad were long and fat, so I quickly spotted my smaller fish closer to the top of the pile. I held my breath as I stepped forward and pulled on its tail with two fingers. It didn't budge. So, I stepped back and exhaled. The fish didn't smell that bad. They smelled like the water of the Potomac. But just the sight of their lifeless bodies, one piled on top of the other, their bluish-green backs reflecting the afternoon sun, made me want to puke.

After three deep breaths, I stepped forward and pushed away some of the fish. My smaller fish slipped off the pile and fell on the ground. Again with two fingers, I tried to pick it up, but it was too heavy. So, I wrapped both hands around its stomach and pulled it toward me. I didn't know what I wanted to do, but I knew I didn't want Papi to make me cut it up and prepare it for dinner. I knew Papi would want me to butcher my little fish first, so I wanted to take it away and hide it.

I took my fish and crawled underneath the back porch. Just below the wooden stairs that led to our back door was a small space I called my fort. It was always dusty and filled with spiderwebs, but it was my safe place. My place, where I could get away from my two other sisters, Patricia and Leticia. I was just small enough to slip through the wooden slats at the side of the stairs. I hid my pocket knife in there, placing my fish in the dirt at the front of my fort and staring down at it. The back door was open, and I heard Mom and Papi inside. I had to do something with my fish, and I knew what I needed was inside in the kitchen.

Carefully, I went into the house and didn't pay any attention to my parents. They were sitting at the kitchen table, and Amelia was standing in the doorway to the dining room. Amelia's arms were crossed as she leaned against the door frame. Minding my own business, I went straight to the cabinet next to the sink and grabbed my mother's pitcher. It was tall and plastic and we usually used it for Kool-Aid or orange juice. I took the pitcher out and started filling it with water. While the water ran, I knew my mother would ask me what I was doing, so I didn't look back at her. I stared at the water, wanting it to fill the pitcher faster, but the faucet was already on full blast.

"Paul!" my mother yelled. "Go outside and play. Go find Patty and Leti and see what they are doing. Your father and I are talking with Amelia, and we don't want to be disturbed."

The pitcher was almost full. I looked at my mother as she ran one hand through her long blond hair. She looked upset, so I shut off the water and took the pitcher outside. I placed my fish in the pitcher and waited to see what would happen. Its head was facing down into the water, so I pulled it out and stuck it back in tail first. Its tail curved at the bottom, and its head leaned up against one side just above the water. Maybe it would soak up the water and be okay. I knew it was not going to come back to life, but I didn't want it to dry out and get all gross. I wanted it to stay small and gray and bluish green, and I didn't want to see its little head chopped off.

I sat back away from the pitcher and crossed my legs. I had just saved my little fish, and I was happy. I reached over beside me, picked up my pocket knife, and opened it. I held the tip of the blade carefully in one hand and threw it straight down into the dirt. But the blade didn't stick. The knife bounced up and landed on its side. So I leaned forward and picked it up.

"Amelia, you're fifteen years old. You don't know anything about life, and you have no idea what you're talking about!" My mother's voice was loud and angry. "How could you be so stupid?" The back door of the house was still open, and I could hear Mom's every word. I imagined her sitting at the kitchen table, pointing her finger at Amelia. Her finger would be shaking in the air as she yelled louder and louder. I adjusted the pocket knife in my hand and closed it carefully.

"Rick and I didn't mean for this to happen. But it did! I'm sorry, but I am old enough to start taking care of myself," Amelia said.

"Oh, great!" Mom yelled. "And how do you plan on taking care of yourself? Tell me that! Is this Rick guy going to quit school and take care of all of you? Are you going to quit school and get a job? You won't be able to work in a few months, and then what?" Mom pounded the table with her fist. I didn't move. I sat perfectly still and listened to every word.

"Rick said he'd help me out as much as he can."

"Is this boy going to marry you, *mija*?" Papi's voice was low and calm. He'd never raise his voice to his daughters, but he yelled at me all the time.

"I don't want to marry Rick! I told you guys that."

"So what? You want us to take care of you and the baby?" My mother's voice grew even louder. "Amelia, I am raising four of my own children, and I am not going to start raising grandchildren just because you can't keep Rick off you!" The room was silent for a second. "Let me tell you, Amelia, you have no idea how much work it can be. You think you're all grown up and you can take care of yourself, but you're still just a child. A stupid little child who knew about sex at the age of seven and should have known better!"

I could hear Amelia crying. My mother always said we were never allowed to call each other stupid. And I couldn't understand why Amelia was stupid. I wanted to run to her and give her a hug; to keep Mom from yelling at her, but I had to take care of my fish. Papi might find it underneath the porch, and I wouldn't be able to protect it and keep its little head from being chopped off. Maybe I could take it back to the Potomac and leave it in the water. Maybe I could sneak it down into the street and throw it in the sewer. I just didn't want Papi to make me cut it up. My fish still looked the same as it lay motionless in the pitcher. I knew I should do something, but instead I sat back and listened to Amelia.

"You don't care!" Amelia yelled. She gasped for air in between her crying. "You're both so mean and selfish and you just don't care!" I could hear her run to her room and slam the door. Amelia always slammed her door. Mom would yell at her again and again, but she'd always slam the door.

I could hear Papi's calm voice, but I didn't listen. My fish looked okay, so I climbed out from underneath the stairs. At the side of our house was a low wall that was made of big concrete blocks. The blocks were thick enough so that I could walk along the top of it. And the wall was low enough so that if I fell off, I could still land on my feet. So I climbed up on top of the wall. I walked over in front of Amelia's bedroom window. I wanted to see if she was okay, but when I got there her window was wide open. I looked down past the front of our house and saw Amelia running down the street. I knew she was mad, so I left her alone. I sat down on the wall and watched her go. I wondered if she was still crying, and before I knew it, she was out of sight.

❖

Dinner was quiet that night. Papi didn't teach me how to clean the fish. He said he was too tired. He put all of the shad back into the cooler and poured ice over them. Mom served us dinner and then stood by the living room window looking for Amelia. I didn't say a word. I didn't tell them I had seen

Amelia running away, and I didn't tell them about my fish under the back porch. I just hoped it wouldn't start to smell. My mom had an amazing sense of smell. Every time I would eat an orange and leave the orange peels in the trash can in my room, she would come in and find them. She'd tell me the peels were stinking up the whole house and I should always put them in the trash can outside. Mom was very strict about stuff like that.

Patty, Leti, and I sat at the dinner table and watched Mom at the window. Papi was back in their bedroom pacing the floor. No one said a word to each other, but I knew we were all praying for Amelia's return and that everything would be the same again.

After dinner, I headed toward the back door to go and check on my fish. But Mom stopped me. "It's too late, Paul. Stay inside and go watch some TV." I hoped my fish would be okay, and I walked to my bedroom to put on my pajamas. When I opened my door, I found Amelia sitting on the floor next to my desk.

"Amelia," I said.

She quickly placed her finger over her mouth and shushed me. I closed the door and lay down on my bed facing her. She was sitting with her legs crossed, and the top drawer of my desk was lying on the floor in front of her. She had pulled the drawer out of my desk and had all of my stuff in small piles around her. My old coins were in one pile. My jacks and marbles were in another, and she was looking through some of the pictures I had cut out of Leti's *Tiger Beat* magazines. Pictures of Lee Majors and Parker Stevenson lay flat on the ground in front of her, and I didn't want her asking me why I kept these pictures hidden in the back of my drawer. Amelia again picked up one of my pictures of the Six Million Dollar Man and examined it closely.

"What are you doing?" I asked. "That's my stuff!"

"Shh!" she said again. "I'm hiding from Mom and Dad. I don't want them to know I'm in here."

I looked up at my window and noticed she had somehow opened it from the outside. "How did you get my window open?"

"Rick helped me," she said with a laugh.

"Rick was here?"

"He sat outside with me for a while, and then he helped sneak me back in." She pressed one of my pictures flat as she laid it down on a pile next to her.

"Amelia, that's my stuff!" She didn't stop. Didn't even look up at me after I yelled at her. Just went on to another one of my pictures. "You and Rick were outside? Why were you and Rick sitting outside?"

"We were watching Mom at the window and Papi as he paced the floor." This time she looked up at me as she pulled another picture from the back of my drawer.

"Amelia, that's my stuff!" I was getting really mad, and I yelled at her louder than I have ever yelled at her before.

"Shut up," she whispered. "And don't be such a little *faggot*." She reached over and hit my hand.

Although no one had ever called me that name before, I knew at the age of seven what it meant. I made my hand into a fist and wanted so bad to hit her back. "Mom and Papi are really mad at you!"

"Paul, shut up. I don't want them to know I'm here."

"I don't care! I want you out of my room and leave my stuff alone." Tears started to well up in my eyes, but I was determined to not cry. "You say Mom and Papi don't care about you, but you don't care about me. You don't care about anyone." I blinked the tears away as best I could. "I don't ever go into your room. Why would I? Patty says you keep your stupid cigarettes in your bottom drawer, but I never go look through your stuff!"

"Mom is gonna come in here now, stupid! You stupid little *faggot*!"

"You're stupid!" I yelled back at her. Everyone in the house could hear me. "Mom called you stupid and she was right. You're stupid! Mom! Mom! Amelia is in my room!"

Amelia slapped my hand again, so I got up and ran to the door. When I opened it, Papi was already outside. With long steps, he walked over to Amelia and grabbed her by the arm. He pulled her to her feet and raised the back of his hand to her. Before he could hit her, he stopped and looked over at me. Papi was angrier than I'd ever seen him before, but he also looked very sad. As he pulled Amelia to her feet and out of my room, he yelled, "Your mother has been so worried, and you're here in Pablo's room. Have you been here the whole time?"

"Papi, you're hurting me!" Amelia was crying again.

"I should hurt you! I should hurt you as much as you hurt me and your mother. That would teach you!" He stopped just outside the door. "Pablo! Did you know she was in here? Did you help her sneak into your room?"

"No, Papi," I said. I too was angry and sad, but my voice was calm. "She said Rick helped her sneak back in, and that they sat outside together and watched you and Mom."

Papi yanked Amelia's arm closer to him. He looked down at me and said, "I'm sorry. I should have known she'd be with that *tonto* boyfriend of hers."

"Papi! She pulled all my stuff from my drawer and left it all over the floor."

"We'll talk about it later, Pablo." Papi pushed Amelia down the hall.

"Amelia." I could hear my mother's voice. "We've been worried sick about you, and you sat outside and watched us worry. What the hell's wrong with you?"

Papi pulled Amelia into their bedroom, and my mother walked past my open door as she followed. Mom then slammed the door, and I could hear my father yelling. I got off the bed. I began to pick up my stuff and put it back into the drawer. When everything was returned to its place, I slid the drawer back into my desk. The whole time I could hear my father yelling and the faint sound of my mother crying. All of this seemed so strange, because my mom was always the one who yelled at Amelia. My father would usually just sit there in silence. I started to cry as I pushed the drawer into the desk. Just as I closed it, I caught my finger in the side. Pain shot through my hand, and I shoved my finger into my mouth. I muffled my crying and tried desperately to stay quiet and listen.

Wanting to find Patty and Leti, I ran from my room and joined them just outside my parents' door. They were crying, too, and my father's voice was growing louder and louder. I wanted to get away, so I ran outside and climbed underneath the back porch. My fish was safe in its plastic pitcher, staring blankly at nothing. It looked completely black in the low light outside. It was beginning to smell. I tried to cover my ears and not listen to my father, but the smell was so bad I placed both hands over my nose. Then I could hear Amelia yelling back at my father, and I could still hear my mother crying. I couldn't take it anymore. Amelia was making my mother cry and I couldn't take it anymore.

I grabbed the pitcher with my fish and climbed out from underneath the stairs. Before going inside, I dumped out about half of the water. My fish fell into the dirt, but I grabbed it and put it back into the half-empty pitcher. Inside the house, I could hear Amelia's voice all around me. Her shouting sounded like she was screeching at the top of her lungs. I couldn't make out what she was saying and I didn't care. I ran past Patty and Leti with the pitcher and opened the door to Amelia's room.

"Paul!" Patty said, and she and Leti followed me into the room.

Once inside, I looked around frantically. Amelia's shouting filled the house, and my ears felt as if they would burst. I gripped the pitcher with one hand and rushed over to Amelia's desk. With the other hand, I pulled her bottom drawer open. Inside there was a large silver ashtray filled with ashes and old cigarette butts. A few packs of cigarettes were around the ashtray with books of matches rubber-banded together. A can of Lysol rolled forward from the back of the drawer.

I listened to Amelia as she shouted and shouted and raised the pitcher up in front of me. Holding it high in the air, I dumped my small fish into the drawer. It made an odd slapping sound as it hit the ashtray. I moved my hands from side to side and emptied out the rest of the water. When the pitcher was completely drained, I looked down at my fish in the middle of a dirty pool of cigarette butts and ashes. I then heard a loud smack from my parent's bedroom, and the house was quiet again.

I turned toward Patty and Leti, who were now standing just outside my parents' door. Everything was quiet and still for a few seconds, and then I could hear my father's calm voice. He talked slowly and quietly to Amelia, but I couldn't hear what he was saying. Patty and Leti moved closer to the door. I walked out of Amelia's room and stood behind my two sisters. After a few seconds, my parents' door opened, and Amelia came out. I looked past her and saw my father sitting on the bed with my mother crying at his side. Her head rested on his shoulder, and his arm was around her back.

Amelia looked at the three of us, but we all stared at our

parents. She walked up to Patty and Leti and bent down to hug them. She wrapped her arms around them, trying to pull their two bodies together, but they pushed her away. Leti looked back at me. I took a step back and looked down at the empty pitcher in my hands. I placed the pitcher on the floor in the hallway and stepped over it. Amelia reached her hand out to touch me, but I slapped it away as she had slapped mine in my bedroom. I carefully walked behind Patty and Leti as we went into my parents' room. We all stood in front of my mother and waited for her to look up at us. She stopped crying, looked at Patty, Leti, and me and smiled. She even laughed a little. I looked away from Mom and stared at Papi. The only thing I could think to say was, "I'm sorry."

Mom continued to laugh through her tears and opened her arms to us. I climbed over behind Papi and hugged him around the neck. Patty crawled up into Mom's lap and Leti sat as close as she could at Mom's side. Mom stopped laughing, but she didn't cry anymore. We all rested our heads against each other and sat perfectly still.

I eventually looked up and saw Amelia standing alone in the hallway. She was crying but didn't make a sound. Large tears rolled down her cheeks, and she wiped them away with the back of her hand. She looked away from us, turned, and walked into her room. She slammed her bedroom door, and Mom jumped when she heard the noise. But the five of us remained silent and still. I pictured Amelia in her bedroom, standing over the open drawer at the bottom of her desk. I closed my eyes and thought of her staring down at her silver ashtray; seeing it filled with dirty water, soggy cigarette butts, and my decaying fish. I closed my eyes tighter, pictured her again, and hoped she was crying.

How I Killed the Governor

I was ten years old in 1977, and I remember sitting in front of the television watching *Super Saturday on NBC*. My father came in with the morning paper and held it up in front of his face as he walked over to the television. I hated it when Dad changed channels. He never watched Saturday morning TV. He'd cut off one of my favorite shows, and I wouldn't be able to watch it again until next Saturday.

Dad stopped his channel search on some news program. My dad always watched the news. It was the only TV he watched. A man with blond hair was just sitting there talking, and my father sat down on the couch next to me. He didn't say a word. Never even apologized for turning the channel. He just folded his newspaper and placed it on the ground in front of him and then sat there and watched the blond guy talk. I thought about going to my room because I hated the news, but I still had to finish my cereal. Maybe it would be over soon.

"Yes. It has been confirmed," the anchorman said. I sat farther back in the couch and sat cross-legged. "Governor Bolin is dead. He died at his home early this morning, and family members say…"

"The governor?" I said, looking back at the TV and then at my dad.

"Yeah, can you believe it?" Dad picked up his paper and read the headline to me. It said the same thing the guy on TV did.

"He's the one?" I looked back at the television and stared at the black-and-white picture of the governor on the screen.

"Yeah," Dad said. "The bastard fired me and then goes and dies three weeks later. How'd ya like that?" He shook his head as he walked back up to the television. "What channel were you watching?"

I turned and stared at nothing. Wesley Bolin. Wesley "Blubber Face" Bolin was dead. I'd told my friends all about him. None of them knew he was the governor and none of them knew Raul Castro was the governor before him.

"What channel were you watching?" my father asked again, this time more insistent.

"*Space:1999*," I blurted out. "Channel five."

My father changed the channel, but it was too late, the credits were already rolling. I'd missed it all, and it wouldn't be on again until next Saturday.

The governor, I thought, as I continued to eat my cereal. The big, bad man that fired my dad and told him he had to leave his office in two weeks. My dad had a big office. It was as big as our living room and our dining room combined. He had a big desk and a phone with a bunch of buttons on it, and he had two secretaries. One was nice, and the other one looked at me like I would break her typewriter if I touched it. I loved typing, and the nice secretary always let me use her typewriter when I came to visit. She was cool, but the other secretary was not. My dad said he always liked the mean one better, but I always liked the nice one. She looked like somebody's mom, but the other lady looked like somebody's grandma.

I turned off the television and took my empty bowl to the kitchen. When I walked through the dining room, I saw the picture of Jesus my parents kept on the back wall. Jesus's face was white and his heart was outside in front of his chest, and it was on fire. His hands had holes in them, and one hand touched his glowing heart while the other one pointed upward, like he was making a peace sign. Jesus looked up at heaven, but I swore for a second, he looked down at me. I almost dropped my cereal bowl. I just stood there and stared at Jesus.

"I didn't mean it," I said. Jesus still looked at heaven, and his hand still touched his glowing heart.

"What are you doing?" My sister Leila stood in the kitchen and laughed at me as I stared at Jesus.

"Nothing." I took my bowl and set it in the sink.

"Were you talking to the picture?" Leila still stood in the center of the kitchen and stared at me.

"No, I was just looking at it." I looked back at Leila for a second and then walked out of the kitchen.

I ran to my bedroom, closed the door, and sat down next to my bed. I had told my best friend, Joey, that I hated Wesley Bolin. He fired my dad, and now we were going to have to move to Tucson. We'd just moved to Phoenix two years ago. Once again, I'd be in a new school. I'd have to make new friends, and I'd have to pack my stuff into a box my mom gave me a couple days ago. The box sat next to me at the foot of my bed. It was still empty. Mom said I had to pack it up today, but I wasn't gonna do it until she made me.

I killed the governor. I told Joey I hated him. Joey told me he hated him, too. I told Joey the governor was fat and ugly, and he didn't know anything because he'd fired my dad. My dad was the nicest guy I knew. Who would fire my dad? What did he ever do wrong?

Dad said Mr. Bolin fired him because he wanted to bring in his own people. That sounded stupid to me. The governor was stupid. He was ugly and stupid, and I thought he should die. I even told God I thought he should die. I prayed God would kill him and we wouldn't have to move. I wouldn't have to leave my friends, and I wouldn't have to pack my stuff. Mom was gonna tell me to pack up my stuff.

"Andrew?" Leila popped her head into my room. "Cartoons are on and—"

"Get out," I yelled, tossing my head back and clenching my fists. She just stayed in the doorway, so I yelled it again. "Get out."

"Don't be such a jerk," Leila said as she closed the door.

She was gonna tell Mom, I thought. She was gonna tell Mom I was a jerk and I killed the governor.

I didn't mean to pray for him to die. I just did it. And Sister Claire at school always said God listens to the prayers of children. God listened to my prayers, and he killed the governor, and I was in big trouble. Mom and Dad would find out, and they'd be mad.

I walked out of my room and closed the door. My mom was washing the breakfast dishes, so I stood behind her and waited for her to finish. She washed the dishes with soap and water and then placed them into the dishwasher. My sister, Tina, who was supposed to wash the dinner dishes, always left the large pan soaking on the counter next to the sink. Mom said she did it so she wouldn't have to clean it herself. Mom sighed heavily and picked up the large pan.

My mom was cool. She always looked like Mrs. Partridge on *The Partridge Family*, except prettier. My mom's hair was always combed and she always smelled like her hairspray. She sprayed her hair for at least ten minutes before we'd leave to go to church. Then my sisters Monica and Adrian began spraying their hair, too. Dad and I always had to wait for them in the car. He'd honk when they took too long and then my mom would come out mad. Sometimes she'd give Dad a little smack on the shoulder and call him "Punchy." Dad would always laugh, and then we'd go to church.

As Mom scrubbed the large pan, I turned and looked over at Jesus. He still stared at heaven, but he looked as if he were smiling. I walked and continued to stare at Jesus. My head rested up against her butt, and I wrapped my arms around her thighs.

"Honey," Mom said after a long sigh.

I still stared at Jesus.

"I'm busy right now. Why don't you go watch TV?" Mom pulled my arms away from her legs with wet hands. She noticed me staring at Jesus, and she looked over at the picture and then back at me. "What, Andrew? Are you all right?"

Mom squatted down in front of me and placed her hand under my chin. She turned my face toward her, but my eyes stayed fixed on Jesus. At any moment, I expected him to wink or give me the thumbs-up. "I took care of your problem, Andrew. Now you won't have to leave your friends." Sister Rafael at school told all of us Jesus was the godfather of all children. I'd just seen that movie with my brother, and now Jesus was scaring me.

I looked at Mom, and my bottom lip began to quiver. "I did something very wrong," I said, and Mom lowered her eyebrows.

"Yeah, he broke the filter on the swimming pool." Leila stood at the end of the breakfast counter and stared at me and Mom.

"You broke the filter," I yelled back, pulling my chin away from Mom's hand and squinting at my sister.

"Did not!"

"Did so!"

"Enough," Mom said. She placed her hands on my shoulders and waited for me to look back at her. "We know you broke the filter, Leila, and we'll talk about that later." Mom looked at me as she spoke.

Leila shut up and ran out of the room.

"Now, what was it you wanted to tell me?"

I looked at Mom and started to cry.

"The governor is dead," I said. "Are we gonna have to move?" I'd stopped crying for a second, and my voice sounded higher.

"Your dad has a new job in Tucson, honey. We talked about this last week. Did you pack that box I left for you in your room?"

I clenched my teeth.

"I didn't pack the box." I started to cry again.

I had to pack the box, and we were still gonna move. So, I'd killed the governor for no reason.

Dad walked into the kitchen and stared down at me.

"What's the matter with him?"

"He's still upset that we have to move." Mom looked at me and held on to my shoulders.

"No," I said, trying to catch my breath. "We...we...we went to church at school last Thursday and...I prayed God would kill the governor." There, it was out. I had made my confession, and I was truly sorry. Sister Claire said that if you were truly sorry for sins, God would always forgive you. God always forgives the sins of children.

"You prayed for God to kill the governor?" they asked together.

I looked up at Dad, and he was trying not to smile. I looked at Mom and she was looking at Dad. They didn't say a thing. They just stared at each other and looked as though they were trying not to laugh at me.

"Let's go sit down in the living room," Mom said.

My father placed his hand behind my back and led me to

the couch. They both sat down next to me. Mom looked at Dad and said, "Why don't you handle this one?" She always said stuff like that when it came to bad grades, or when I finally hit Leila back, and she'd go straight to Mom telling her I needed a spanking.

I looked at Dad, and he just smiled.

"Andrew," he began. "God doesn't listen to the prayers of children when they pray for grownups to die. He just doesn't work that way."

"But I prayed for the governor to die, and now he's dead."

"The paper this morning said the governor died of a heart attack. It's probably a problem he's had for a very long time." Dad put his hand on my shoulder. "I'm sure your prayers had nothing to do with Mr. Bolin dying. It was just his time to go. Besides, God wouldn't kill someone just because you asked him to. He has much nicer prayers to answer."

"Are you sure?" I looked at Mom and then back at Dad.

"Your dad's sure, honey," Mom said, smiling at Dad. "Your dad went to high school with Jesus. He knows him very well." My dad went to high school with Santa Claus, too.

I was off the hook. My parents didn't think I'd killed the governor, and that was good enough for me. When we were finished, Mom told me to go to my room and pack my stuff into that box.

Slowly I placed my Hardy Boys books and my track ribbons into the box. Leila slipped her head into my room. "Hey, stupid, heard you killed Blubber Face."

I turned my head and stared at her. She didn't leave, so I got down on my knees, closed my eyes, and placed my hands together.

"What are you doing?" she asked.

"I'm talking to God about you."

FATHER TEPSIK AND THE AVENGING ANGEL

My Grandpa Shipman sits next to me in a folding chair on the front porch of his house in Tucson. Ruth, my grandfather's second wife, is busy washing the dinner dishes inside. I look up at my grandfather from where I sit on the front step and watch him as he takes a bite of his Fudgie Pop. I put down the naked wooden stick of my own Fudgie Pop next to me on the step.

The evening is hot and dry, and my grandfather waits patiently for the summer sun to set over the Rincon Mountains. For the first time in my weekend visit, I have him all to myself. His wife's chair sits empty next to him. She is not there to complain about her bad back or how the neighbors play their stereo too loud. She is not sitting there telling me all about her own grandson, and how she would love for the two of us to meet.

She's always saying how much the two of us have in common. We're both ten years old, he has two sisters, while I have four, and we both go to Catholic school. He lives back East, while I live in Phoenix, and Ruth says the next time he comes out for a visit, she would love to have me come down again. Ruth is nice. She just talks way too much.

My grandfather looks over at the mountains and then down at me.

"It's summertime, Andrew. The sun won't be setting for at least another hour."

"That's okay, Grandpa." I smile back at him. "We're not going anywhere."

Grandpa laughs because he taught me that saying. When somebody asks him how his car is running, he always replies, "It hasn't left me standing." Or when someone else asks him a difficult question regarding politics or history, he always turns to me and says, "Must have been absent from junior high that day." My grandfather is famous for his one-liners, but I hadn't realized until I came for my visit this weekend that his wife always interrupts him and never gives him a chance to talk. All my grandfather can do is form sentences that are no longer than six or seven words. After that, his wife always jumps in and takes over.

Before I left for my visit, my mother told me to ask Grandpa about his teacher when he was a young boy. "Ask him about Father Tepsik and the one-room schoolhouse in West Bridgewater," Mom said as she packed a few of my clothes into my green backpack.

With Ruth busy inside the house, I knew now would be the best time to hit up Grandpa for one of his old stories. He'd already told me how he and his friends burned some rotten eggs in the high school incinerator when he was a teenager. They stunk up the whole building, so the high school was let out early to be aired out. He'd also told me a couple of stories about him and my grandmother, and how she died just one month before I was born.

My grandmother knew that I was going to be a boy, and she kept telling my grandpa how excited she was. After giving birth to four daughters, my mom was ready for a boy. My grandma said the timing was right, and she had a dream where God told her to expect a grandson. She fell and broke her hip after her annunciation dream, and a piece of her bone traveled up through her body and pierced her heart. My grandma died while my mother lay sick in bed during her pregnancy, and when my father called Grandpa to tell him Mom had given birth to a baby boy, Grandpa simply replied, "Yeah, I knew it'd be a boy."

The telephone rings inside the house, and I turn around to look through the screen door. Ruth walks into the living room and sits down in her chair. She answers the phone, and it sounds like she is talking to her daughter, who also lives in Phoenix.

"Grandpa?" I look over at him and watch him feed his brown poodle, Buttons, what's left of his Fudgie Pop. "My mom told me to ask you about Father Tepsik. She said you'd tell me a story about him. Do you remember that story, Grandpa?"

"I never told you the story of Father Tepsik?" Grandpa leans forward in his chair and looks over his shoulder into the living room. He sees Ruth on the phone and turns back toward me. "Sit up here, Andrew." He pats his hand on the seat of Ruth's chair. "And I'll tell you all about good old Father Tepsik."

As I sit down in the chair, both of us turn and watch Ruth as she talks on the phone. I hope she'll be occupied for at least a while, and I think Grandpa feels the same way.

My grandfather looks out at the road in front of his house and sighs. "Well. When I was about your age, I went to Catholic school, too. 'Cept I was Baptist, and it was really the only school in town. It was a one-room schoolhouse like you see in the old movies, and our teacher was a white-haired priest by the name of Father Tepsik."

Grandpa closes his eyes and shakes his head. "He was a real son of a bitch." Grandpa laughs as he looks down at my shocked expression. "You see, Andrew, back in the old days, it would get really cold in the wintertime in Massachusetts. Old Father Tepsik would always warm himself in the morning by taking two students back into the cloakroom and spanking them with his wooden paddle. It was made from a dark brown wood, and it was about yea long." Grandpa holds two fingers out in front of him and stretches them about two feet apart.

"He'd paddle one of the younger students first, then finish up on either me or my two friends, Ray and Jacob, because we were the oldest and tallest kids in the class. It soon got to be a rotation between the three of us. Me first, then Raymond, then Jacob. If Father Tepsik ever forgot the rotation, he'd always ask us whose turn it was. Of course, we'd always tell the truth and take our turn in the cloakroom. By the time he'd finish, he'd be all nice and warm and ready to start his lesson."

"Didn't you tell your parents your teacher was spanking you so much?" I ask, watching my grandfather lean forward in his chair.

"Oh, we told our parents, and they always said that a little discipline was good for us older boys. Things were different in those days, Andrew. You never questioned a priest, and you always did what the teacher told you to do."

"Sister Raphael, our principal, she has a paddle she uses on the bad kids. I've never been paddled 'cuz I always stay away from Sister Raphael." I stop and wait, and my grandfather smiles.

"Well, Father Tepsik had it in for the three of us, and as the winter turned colder, our asses got sorer. So we decided to do something about it.

"You see, Andrew, Father Tepsik always told us stories from the Old Testament about the unforgiving God. He said if God truly wanted to punish someone for his sins, God would send an avenging angel to do his work for him. 'Revenge' was one of Father's favorite words. He told us God would send an avenging angel to seek revenge on any evil man who wronged a Christian person. Father also told us you could always tell when an avenging angel came down from heaven and helped you out due to the strong scent of roses left behind. As children, we all believed what Father Tepsik told us, so we waited for an avenging angel to come and help us out. We prayed day and night, and we actually thought an angel had been sent to the schoolhouse one time." Grandpa turns his head and looks back inside. Ruth is still on the phone, so he straightens himself in his chair.

"Once, when Jacob was the one taken back into the cloakroom, we thought God had finally sent an avenging angel to punish old Father Tepsik. When Father had finished on Jacob and Missy Jones, I think, they walked out of the cloakroom, and you could see the Father's face was all sweaty and red from the excitement of paddling Jacob. Father Tepsik always kept a portrait of himself hanging behind his desk in the old schoolhouse. It was a photograph of him in his white collar with a big silver cross hanging around his neck. He was posed to one side with his right hand touching his big ole cross, thinking he was all saintly or something." Grandpa takes his hand and places it just below his neck, turning his head toward me as he rolled his eyes.

"Well, when he and Jacob walked out of the cloakroom, Father Tepsik's portrait fell to the ground and cracked its wooden frame. When Jacob saw it hit the floor, he turned to me and Raymond and said, 'It's the avenging angel.' Father Tepsik turned around and shot him the most evil glare I think I've ever seen. It could have been an avenging angel, for all we knew, but we sure as hell didn't smell any roses.

"On our way home that afternoon, all three of us got to talking about how we thought it might have been an avenging angel who made Father's picture fall off the back wall. But I kept telling them I couldn't smell a damn thing after the portrait hit the ground. Raymond said he didn't smell it either, 'cuz his mom had this perfume that smelled exactly like fresh roses. His dad bought it for her at Christmas, and Raymond said he hated that damn perfume 'cuz it made his mom smell like the church garden. Well, when Raymond mentioned the rose-smelling perfume, I got an idea. I told them if we were tired of waiting around for some avenging angel to come and help us with Father Tepsik, then we might as well help ourselves." Grandpa leans in closer to me and waves his pointed finger in the air. "If Father Tepsik thought an avenging angel was after him, he'd surely straighten up and stop beatin' us all the time."

The sound of the screen door opening interrupts Grandpa. We both turn our heads and see Ruth standing inside the door looking down at me in her chair.

"That was Gertrude," Ruth says, still holding on to the doorknob. "She's doing fine and sends her best." She stays in the doorway, expecting me to move out of her chair.

"Good," Grandpa replies. "Are you gonna bake that angel food cake you threatened us with this morning?" Grandpa turns his eyes toward me, then rolls them back up at Ruth. "You told Andrew he could have it for dessert tomorrow night."

"Oh yeah." Ruth nods her head forward and smiles. "I'll bake that right now so he can have it for breakfast tomorrow morning. That sound good?" Ruth looks down at me.

"Sure," I said. I really don't like angel food cake, but I know Ruth has some fresh strawberries, so I widen my eyes and shake my head.

"Now, where was I?" Grandpa says after the screen door slams shut.

"The rose perfume." I watch my grandpa as he nods and looks out toward the road.

"Well, Raymond said he was gonna steal his mother's perfume, and I said I was gonna stay home sick from school the next day. With all of us working together, we were gonna help Father Tepsik believe there was an avenging angel after him. That was gonna be me. So, I went home and I got an egg from my mother's icebox and blew it hollow." Grandpa stops and turns toward me. "You know how to blow an egg hollow?"

"Yeah," I say, pretending to hold an egg in my left hand. "You take a pin and poke a hole at the top of the egg, and then another hole at the bottom, and then you blow the white and yellow stuff out." I blow into my imaginary egg.

"Well, once I had the egg hollow, I glued a pebble to one end, filled the egg with some of my mother's kerosene, and glued another pebble to the top. In the morning, I told my mom I had a stomachache and stayed home from school. Before school started, I snuck out my bedroom window and met Jacob and Raymond behind the schoolhouse. They helped me up on the roof, and I crawled over and lay next to the smoke pipe. When Father Tepsik came to school that day, he took Raymond back into the cloakroom, 'cuz it was his day to go, and Jacob got out of his seat and waited for them by the iron stove. The potbelly stove heated the schoolhouse, but obviously not enough." Grandpa stops and looks over at the lowering sun.

"When Father Tepsik came out of the cloakroom that day, he saw Jacob out of his seat, and he yelled his name really loud. '*Jacob!*' He'd always yell Jacob's name really loud, and we all said it was because he thought he was quoting the Bible or preachin' during some Sunday service. Fire and brimstone kinda stuff." Grandpa laughs. "Well, him yelling Jacob's name was my signal, so I took my kerosene-filled egg and dropped it down the pipe into the potbelly stove. Jacob told me when it hit, the explosion blew open the front door of the stove with black smoke shootin' out into the schoolhouse. When Father Tepsik saw the door fly open, Raymond pulled his mother's perfume out of his pocket and squirted a bunch of it into the air." Grandpa laughs some more and shakes his head. "Once I let go of that egg, I climbed down from the roof and ran as fast as I could. I tell you, I have never ran so fast in my life.

"Well, Raymond managed to squirt the perfume and hide the bottle back in his pocket before Father Tepsik was able to turn around. And when Father smelled the roses all around him, Jacob said, 'It's an avenging angel.' Father Tepsik got pretty scared, but not scared enough to stop beatin' us. When I came to school the next day, Father Tepsik walked in at eight o'clock and took me and someone else, back into the cloakroom. We thought he'd be convinced that an angel was after him but he tanned my hide nice and red that morning."

Grandpa turns his head and looks at me. "We thought he might have figured out what we had done, so we laid low for just a few days. But the weather kept gettin' colder and the paddling kept gettin' harder." Grandpa leans down closer to me again. "So, one day when I'm in the cloakroom with Father Tepsik, I thought of another way to trick him with the rose perfume. You see, in the old schoolhouse there was this cabinet Father Tepsik used to stock the firewood in. It had a door that opened outside, next to the wood pile, and a door that opened inside, at the back of the cloakroom. So Father could always pull out some wood during the day and throw it into the potbelly stove. Well, after school that day, I took a big chance and asked Raymond for the bottle of rose perfume. He had it hidden in the woods behind the schoolhouse, so we went and got it, and I told them I had another plan." Grandpa sits up straight in his chair and leans his head back.

"Father Tepsik stayed after school until around five

o'clock, so I snuck into the wood cabinet, while Jacob and Raymond watched Father through the side window. If anything went wrong, they would distract him, and I'd just have to get myself out of the wood cabinet. Well, sure enough, Jacob checked on Father and knocked once on the cabinet door after he'd seen him sitting at his desk reading.

"With Father busy at his desk, I snuck into the schoolhouse and took the wooden paddle off its hook in the cloakroom. I can't believe I did this, but I took my old pocket knife and cut the tip of my finger so I could cover the paddle with blood. Once I got it all good and covered, I squirted a bunch of the rose perfume up in the air and then snuck back into the wood cabinet. Before I shut the door, I threw the paddle up in the air, and it made a loud smack when it hit the ground. Being a stupid young kid, I stayed in the cabinet and watched Father Tepsik rush back into the cloakroom and pick up the wooden paddle. Once he had it in his hands, he noticed the blood on the handle and all over the floor and on his hands. Father looked around to see if anyone was there, and just before he looked over at the wood cabinet, he took a deep breath and smelled all of the rose perfume."

Grandpa places his hand over his eyes and laughs once again. "Like a shot, he fell down onto his knees and started praying to the Virgin Mary. I guess he'd figured he'd pissed off God, so he prayed to Mary to see if she could bail him out. Father Tepsik just kept praying." Grandpa clears his throat and lowers his voice. "'Virgin Mary, mother of God, pray for us sinners, pray for us sinners.' I tell you, I could barely keep myself quiet in that wood cabinet. I was laughing so hard, and I knew Father Tepsik would never use that damn paddle on us again."

Grandpa looks over at me and then raises his head to see if Ruth is still working in the kitchen.

"But what happened to Father Tepsik, Grandpa?" I lean my head forward and place it in front of his face.

"Let me tell you the rest of the story." Grandpa crosses his legs. "Me, Raymond, and Jacob run into Father Tepsik as he's walking out of church that next Sunday, and he calls us over before we had a chance to run away. He's all dressed up in his black suit, and he's got this big old carpetbag with him. He ends up telling us we don't have school next week because he's leaving town, but we should have a new schoolteacher by the end of next week. We all just stood there with our mouths hanging wide open, and he told us to be good students and to mind our new teacher. When he walked away, all three of us were still just standing there. We watched old Father Tepsik go, and we couldn't believe our luck."

Grandpa straightens his back, opens his mouth, and shows me what he must have looked like back then. "I turned to Raymond and smiled, and then I turned to Jacob and laughed. All three of us must have laughed for about a good two minutes. I then stopped, turned to Raymond, and smacked him on his arm. I said, 'Ray, quit spraying that dang perfume everywhere.' I swear I could smell it all around me. Even Jacob said he could smell it. But Raymond stopped laughing and stared right back at me. He said, 'I don't have the perfume. I put it back on my mother's dresser two days ago.'

"Well, the smell of roses was everywhere, and Raymond, Jacob, and I got all scared, so we ran into Father Tepsik's church and kneeled down together in the back pew. I tell ya, we were so scared, we didn't know what to do. Raymond kept telling us he didn't have the perfume, and he even pulled out his pockets to show us they were empty. We prayed in the back of that church for at least an hour. I thanked God for taking Father Tepsik away, and then I asked for a nice young teacher to come and replace him." Grandpa stops and looks down at me again.

"Ya think God helped you get rid of Father Tepsik?"

"I don't know." Grandpa looks back into the house.

"Mom always says that you were a little devil when you were a kid."

"Oh, I was a devil all right. But sometimes even an angel has to be a little devilish." Grandpa turns away and laughs. "You know what I mean, Andrew?"

"I think so."

The opening of the screen door stops our conversation. This time it slams shut, and Ruth is standing in front of us on the porch. As she wipes her hands on the front of her apron, I jump up from her chair. "I'm sorry, Ruth, you can have your chair back now. I'll sit down here." I sit down on the step in front of my grandpa.

"What have you two been talking about?" Ruth asks after she lowers herself into her folding chair next to Grandpa.

"Grandpa told me how he was a little angel when he was my age." I smile at my grandfather and watch him turn his eyes away from his wife.

"I don't think I've ever been an angel, Andrew," Grandpa says.

"Oh, you sure haven't," Ruth replies with a laugh.

"But everyone runs into an angel at least once in his life, Andrew." Grandpa leans over toward Ruth and stares into her eyes. "I've just been lucky, and I got to marry my angel." He presses his lips forward, and Ruth gives him a little kiss.

"You are sure full of it today, Shipman," Ruth says as she sits back in her chair.

Grandpa and I both laugh and listen to Ruth as she starts in with her complaining about her many aches and pains. She says her arthritis hasn't been bothering her as much due to all of the cooking she's been doing since I arrived. The smell of the angel food cake baking in the kitchen is sweet and warm, and the sun is just beginning to set over the Rincon Mountains. As I sit back and watch it, I rest my hand on the top of my grandfather's shoe. Grandpa and I then sit quietly and ignore Ruth as she goes on and on about her daughter and how she never has time to come down for a visit.

A Kiss Between Altar Boys

I had my first kiss when I was thirteen years old. It took place outside of St. Patrick's Church in the priest's garden. It wasn't really a garden but a half-dead patch of Bermuda grass surrounded by five or six orange trees. The trees had dark green leaves, withered-looking oranges that never produced juice, and trunks painted bright white from the ground to the point in each tree where it began to branch out. And the kiss was not with a young girl, but my best friend, Liam, who was also thirteen years old. We had just finished serving mass as altar boys at St. Patrick's in downtown Tucson and it was an extremely brave moment for two of the most popular boys in school at the time.

It was the last day of school in 1980, when we were both in the sixth grade. Summer vacation was about to begin, and like every last day at our Catholic grade school, we ended the year with a celebratory mass. Father O'Leary officiated that day, and Liam and I served as altar boys. This was back when altar boys had a great deal of responsibility during mass: from washing the priest's hands after the gospel to ringing the bells when the Eucharist was consecrated and holding small saucers under the chins of parishioners as the body of Christ is placed on their tongues. We were also required to wear black pants hemmed to hang right above the black laces of our beautifully polished black shoes.

Liam and I were the best of the trained altar boys at St. Patrick's at the time, and Father O'Leary always requested we serve him when he celebrated mass. This was due to the fact that both Liam and I were redheads, and Father O'Leary said we looked like three Irish lads serving our loving God. Liam Seaver and Father Sean O'Leary, of course, were Irish, while I, Ernesto Quintanilla, was not.

I am Mexican-American with both of my great grandfathers immigrating to the United States from Mexico at the turn of the century. My red hair comes from my Mexican heritage, and I believe nothing about my appearance or coloring makes me look Irish. At least, I don't see it that way. But people always see my red hair and automatically assume I'm Irish. They tend to overlook my jet black eyes and dark brown skin and see my auburn hair as a product of Ireland. While I would consider Liam to be a *ginger*, with his pale white skin, freckles around the nose, and red hair almost the color of a shiny copper penny, I am more of what I would call a burgundy or a darker shade of red.

For Liam and me, being redheads really bonded us as best friends at a very young age. With all of the bullying and teasing that takes place even in Catholic grade schools, Liam and I were often called "carrot top" or "fire crotch" or "orangutan" and always at Christmas time one of us was referred to as "Heat Miser." Classmates would often walk behind us during the winter months and pretend to warm their cold hands at the tops of our heads. Which is not very amusing for a *ginger* and a *burgundy*. The older we got, the more sophisticated the name calling became. Eventually our classmates realized Liam was Irish and I was Mexican, so Liam became the "Red Mick" while I became the "Red Spic."

So that day at the end of sixth grade, we sat together on a short wall behind the church. The wall was constructed of thick concrete blocks, and it was no higher than three feet tall. It surrounded the priest's garden, which was located between the back door of the church and the front door of the rectory. It was late in the afternoon and all of the other students had gone home after mass while Liam and I helped Father O'Leary close up the church. When we were done and Father O'Leary had said goodbye for the summer, Liam and I sat together and watched the remaining teachers load up their cars and drive away.

"You gonna work this summer?" Liam asked.

"Yeah, I start next week. My cousin's gonna train me as a busboy at my uncle's restaurant."

"La Fonda, right? On the west side?"

"Yeah. Mexican food and margaritas. That's my life this summer. What about you?"

"Gonna go and spend some time with my grandparents in New York."

"Nice. Get out of the heat."

Liam looked over at me and raised one eyebrow. "So, you got four sisters, right?"

"Yeah. Two at St. Mary's and two at the university. I'm the youngest."

"They redheads, too?"

"Nah. They all got brown hair. I'm the only redhead."

"I think it's weird that you're a red."

"I think it's weird that you're red, too."

Liam smiled. He looked me right in the eyes and for the first time did not turn away. He kept staring at me. I didn't know what to do, but I knew I didn't want to look away. I'd never stared Liam in the eyes before, and I couldn't believe how fucking blue they were. They weren't too dark or too light; they were an in-between blue. And as he continued to stare at me, I began to feel an uncomfortable churning in my stomach. I felt like I was gonna throw up, so I turned away and closed my eyes. All I could see was the blue of Liam's eyes. I shook my head, trying to think of something else.

I knew Liam came from a strict Irish Catholic family, and his dad worked for the city as a garbage man. He was one of those guys who rode on the fender of a garbage truck and dumped the trash cans into the back. Liam was the middle child in his family, with an older brother who was out of high school but always in trouble with the law, and a younger sister who was also at St. Patrick's in the fourth grade. His mom was a beautiful woman with short blond hair and looked a lot like Audra Barkley, or Linda Evans, on the TV show *The Big Valley*.

"You okay?" Liam asked.

"Yeah," I replied, feeling my stomach returning to normal. But as I opened my eyes, I watched Liam scoot down the wall and sit closer to me. We were a few inches apart and I stared down at our knees, which were now just about touching each other.

"You know," Liam began. "My brother was telling me about this movie that's out that's all about fags. It's got that guy Al Pacino in it. You know, from *The Godfather*."

"Al Pacino?" I asked, trying to think of who he was in *The Godfather*.

"Yeah, it's all about these bars in New York where guys go to have sex with other guys. Doesn't that sound just sick?"

"Yeah, sick." His eyes were wide open as he stared at me, and he had a bright smile covering his face. "Have you seen the movie?" I asked.

"No." He stopped with a short laugh. "My brother saw it. He told me about it. But can you imagine?"

"What? Guys having sex with other guys? Is that what you're asking me about?"

"Yeah." Liam stopped laughing. "What? Why are you getting so serious? I was just joking with you."

"I just think it's weird you'd wanna see a movie like that."

"I didn't say I wanted to see the movie. I just thought it was weird."

"Yeah, weird," I said. "Everything's weird these days." I don't know why I said that. I just did. And when it was out there, I wished I could take it back, but I couldn't. So I decided to let those words hang out there until Liam said something else.

Liam exhaled loudly and looked away from me. "I know," he said. "Everyone calls you weird."

"Yeah. And everyone calls you weird, too."

"They do?"

"Yeah, they do. It's not just me they call weird. Fuck, everyone at this school is weird."

Liam turned away and laughed again.

"What?" I said.

"You never use the word 'fuck.' So, that was really funny."

"I know. I'm a good fucking altar boy."

"We're both good fucking altar boys."

Then without looking over or prompting each other, we both said, "We're both weird fucking altar boys."

While I thought this was funny and laughed out loud, Liam found it hilarious and laughed so hard he fell back on the ground behind the short wall. With his feet sticking up in the air, his shoes at the top of the wall, and his back flat on the grass behind the wall, Liam continued to laugh. And as I watched him grab his stomach and howl even louder, I began to laugh harder and fell back beside him.

We both lay on the ground with our feet in the air and

laughed for another minute or two. It wasn't that what we said was so funny; it was that we were having such a good time together. We always agreed with one another and knew how to make each other laugh. When we stopped laughing, I thought about reaching over and smacking Liam in the stomach, but he was holding my hand at his side. I wasn't aware he had grabbed my hand. Although I was shocked, I decided to let it be and see what happened.

Again, I looked Liam in the eyes. I had never felt this combination of fear and excitement, and this time the feeling went much lower than my stomach. I knew I should probably lie on the ground for a few more minutes and calm myself down. Liam looked back at me and didn't say a thing. Without a word, I grasped his hand tighter. He looked as if he finally realized we were holding hands. He lifted his shoulder, leaned over, and kissed me on the mouth, his lips pressing against mine without knowing what to do next. Our heads remained together for a few seconds, but the kiss was like our two hands, pressing up against each other without any movement.

When Liam finally moved away and rested back down on the ground, he said, "That was not very good." He laughed.

"Then let's try it again," I said, lifting my shoulder. I moved my head over his, separated our hands, and held his face steady. Doing what my older sister had made me practice on a picture of Farrah Fawcett, I kissed him on the mouth. I tilted my head to one side, opened my mouth, and pushed my tongue up against his. When I felt him relax and respond, I let my tongue caress his, and it became a deep and intimate kiss. When I pulled away, he smiled up at me, and then we both looked around ourselves, forgetting where we were and what we were doing.

The priest's garden was still deserted, and no one had seen us kiss each other. The wall that surrounded the garden also provided additional cover, so if anyone was in the parking lot or on the street across from the church, they couldn't have seen us. We knew we were safe and still alone. So, we rested our heads back down on the ground and held hands once again.

When the silence had become unbearable, and we knew we had to say something to each other, we heard a car honking its horn as it drove past the back wall of the priest's garden.

"Shit," Liam said. "That's my mom. She always honks her horn till I come out and find where she's parked."

"Shit." I picked myself up off the ground.

As we both slowly crouched upward past the top of the wall, we saw Liam's mom's car parked farther down at the front of the church. She honked her horn once again, this time much longer, and looked around for Liam.

Standing up, I noticed dead grass at the top of Liam's hair and brushed it off with the side of my hand. Without meaning to, I noticed I was also straightening his collar and making sure that he looked presentable for his mother. I stopped what I was doing and realized I had somehow become the caring girlfriend who needed to stop primping her boyfriend. I lowered my hands in front of me and held them together, which also hid a bit of my remaining excitement.

Liam laughed at me. "I gotta go," he said, adjusted the front of his pants, and continued to stare at me the way he had all afternoon. "So, I'll see you next year?"

"Yeah. See you next year."

He turned and hopped back over the wall. But before he could turn away and rush to his mother, he said, "What about your ride? Will your mom be here soon?"

"No, I'm walking home. You know…I just live down the street about four blocks away."

"So, what?" Liam smiled brightly. "You waited around just to hang out with me?"

"Yeah. I guess."

Liam looked over at his mother's car. She was still staring at the front door of the church. He looked back at me, grabbed my arm, and pulled me toward him, kissing me quickly on the mouth. With a smile, he let go of me and rushed over to his mother. Watching him run, I hopped over the short wall and stood silent on the other side. Thinking of next year, I smiled to myself, turned away from the church, and headed for home.

Slipping from Grace

The restaurant was quiet and the coffee was strong—everything Grace had hoped to find this afternoon. She was tired of sitting, but she knew she'd look ridiculous standing in front of the window drinking her coffee. She tried not to care what she looked like, but she slumped back down in her chair and raised the cup to her lips.

Grace was seated at the front of the restaurant, one table away from the large window that faced 2nd Street. It was a small place in the middle of downtown, a good two miles away from the hospital. Grace had walked by the place several times while running errands, but she had never stopped in for lunch. It was much more of a diner, with a lunch counter and short booths upholstered with Naugahyde. The front window advertised a daily special of coffee and a chicken salad sandwich for $4.99. Grace could only work up her appetite for the cup of coffee. She stared down into her cup: black with two packages of Sweet'n Low. She blew into the cup as she placed it back down on the table.

Outside the front window, Grace saw two teenage girls. Both looked feminine, with small cheekbones and pale white skin. Their eyes were outlined with blue and purple eye shadow, and their hands looked skeletal with long fingernails covered in shiny black polish. Grace looked down at the white socks pulled up to just below their knees. *They're not different*, Grace thought. "They're exactly the same," she whispered to herself.

She remembered her own wardrobe as a teenager and how her mother hated her long, straight hair. Every other morning before school, Grace would wash her long hair, wrap it around her head, pin it down, and cover it with a hair net. An hour and ten minutes of sitting under the hair dryer usually did the trick. She would then emerge with her somewhat straightened hair; the perfect style for a teenager of the seventies. Grace ran her hand up the back of her head. Her short hair felt prickly even though it hadn't been washed in two days. "Mama always hated my hair," she whispered to herself again.

"Did you want more coffee, hon?" The waitress stopped at her side. She held the coffeepot up in front of her, and Grace noticed her name tag. Fran.

"Yes, please." Grace pushed her cup closer to the edge of the table. Looking at the waitress, Grace tried to find some element of the woman's appearance that reminded her of someone she knew. Fran's red hair had obviously come from a bottle, and her wrinkled face appeared to be covered with a powder that was the exact same color. *The woman is practically burgundy*, Grace thought. Fran had dark, attentive eyes that scanned her tables while she poured Grace more coffee. Even her short body and heavy bosom did not remind Grace of anyone. She thanked Fran for the fresh cup.

At the front of the restaurant sat a dirty table. Grace had not seen the people get up and leave, but she was glad they were now gone. She had a better view of 2nd Street, and she searched outside to see if she could find her son. *No, that's wrong*, she thought. She closed her eyes and exhaled. Her son, Sean, was no longer her son. He was her daughter, Shauna, and

Grace was still getting used to the transition—the new clothes, the new school, the new makeup, and the new pronoun. Her, Grace thought. She was looking for her. Shauna. She looked around to see if she could see her daughter, Shauna.

Shauna wanted to spend the afternoon shopping with friends, and Grace had told her to stop by the diner at four o'clock. Grace looked down at her watch. It was 3:43. She had time to drink her coffee and try to relax. She hoped she would at least see Shauna walking by, laughing with her friends and enjoying herself. Grace placed her elbows on the table and sat up straight in her chair. She leaned forward, thinking she would have a better view around the street corner, but it was all the same.

As Grace continued to search the street, a young boy walked up to the table in front of her and began to stack the dirty dishes. He was a heavy kid, and he stepped from one side of the table to the other, piling the silverware into an empty glass. Grace lowered her shoulders. The kid was in her way, and she could not see around him. She sat farther back and placed her right foot up on the chair next to her.

Grace watched the waitress walk past her table. "Thanks, kid," Fran said as she walked up to the table, piled the dirty dishes onto one arm, and stuck her fingers down into the four water glasses. The young boy smiled at the waitress, brushed off two of the chairs, and sat down. Grace turned and saw a young woman, younger than Grace but obviously the boy's mother. She stepped away from the front door and sat down next to her son. The young woman removed her sunglasses and placed them on the table. She pulled a black case out of her purse and put on a regular pair of glasses. She slipped the sunglasses into the black case and placed it back into her purse.

The young boy sat at the table and looked pleased with himself. He smiled as he watched the waitress walk away. He looked at his mother, smiled, and then looked over and saw Grace. He stared at her for a second and turned away with a more serious expression. Grace looked down at her coffee cup. Her spoon rested next to her hand, and she noticed a brown spot underneath it. She pushed the spoon aside and rubbed the mark with the tip of her finger.

Grace continued to look for Shauna out the front window, but the young boy kept coming into her view. He was not a small child. He was ten or eleven, Grace thought, and probably a good thirty pounds overweight. He had short, thick arms, and Grace noticed his large shoe size. He'll probably have a growth spurt in the next two years and become a very big man, Grace thought. The young boy held his head down looking at his menu, but Grace could see his eyes looking up at her. Again, she realized she was staring at him for no reason, and she quickly turned her head away.

"Did you want to order some food, hon?" Fran stood next to the table. She held up her ticket book and pulled her pen out of her apron.

"I don't..." Grace looked up into her face, and Fran smiled down at her. Her smile reminded Grace of her mother. Her mother was taller than Fran. She had blond hair that was usually combed back into a neat bun, and she wore glasses. But her mother's smile always revealed her one crooked tooth, and Fran definitely had a similar smile. Most of Fran's teeth were crooked and yellow, probably from years of smoking, but her smile had some brightness, too. Grace laughed to herself and said, "I think I'll try the chicken salad. Is it any good?"

"Ah, hon, it's the best." Fran wrote the order in her book. She smiled down at Grace again. Grace quickly turned away, happy to see the resemblance to her mother. She glanced up after hearing the young mother at the next table laughing. Grace watched the young mother tilt her head back and place her hand on her son's shoulder. *Her son is making her laugh*, Grace thought. The young boy's shoulders moved up and down as he laughed along with his mother. He looked over at Grace for a second, then turned his head back toward his mother and continued to laugh.

"That's so funny," the young mother said rather loudly. She still had her hand on her son's shoulder, and Grace watched to see if the young boy would jerk away from her touch. Grace stared intently at the woman's hand, but it didn't move. Grace wanted the boy to lean back in his chair and break away from his mother. But they just continued to laugh. Grace turned away. She looked down the wall next to her.

The string of bells that hung from the front door rang. Grace saw her daughter, Shauna, walking into the restaurant. Shauna looked around at the first few tables and then spotted her mother. Shauna's expression was stern, and she stared at the wall as she walked over to the table. Grace sat up straight again as her daughter sat down in the chair next to her. Shauna didn't say a word. She didn't even look at her mother. She just sat down and brushed her strawberry blond bangs away from her eyes.

Grace stared at Shauna's face and smiled a bit at the progress she could see in her daughter's appearance. Sean no longer sat before her. She was Shauna, with her perfectly shaped eyebrows, her clean-looking makeup that covered up anything even remotely still masculine, and her thick, long hair. Only a light rinse with a bit of henna was needed to transform Shauna into the fierce Irish ginger she had become. And all that remained of Sean was his Adam's apple. It was the only thing that reminded Grace of the sensitive little boy still somewhere inside this fiery teenage girl.

Grace looked up and her eyes met those of the young boy at the next table, who now sat quietly with his mother. Grace looked into his serious expression and then turned back toward her daughter.

"Did you buy anything?" she asked Shauna.

"I bought some clothes." Shauna continued to stare down at the table.

"I just ordered a sandwich. Would you like anything?"

"No." Shauna reached over and picked up the salt shaker. "Actually I thought…" She looked over at her mother. "Never mind."

"What?" Grace asked. She had pulled her hand up to touch her daughter's arm, but she dropped it to her side.

"Never mind," Shauna said in a louder tone.

Grace looked down at the table and was surprised to see Fran placing her plate down in front of her. She laughed at how her heart had jumped.

"There's your food, hon."

"Thank you," Grace replied, placing her hand on her chest. She continued to smile as she looked up at Fran and then over at the young boy. He was laughing again with his mother, and Grace waited for him to look up at her. When he did, she smiled at him, and he smiled back.

"Did you want some food, hon?" Fran asked Shauna.

Grace looked over at her daughter. "Get some dinner, honey. This sure beats that hospital food any day."

"No."

"You been in the hospital, hon?" Fran looked down at Shauna and then over at Grace.

"No," Grace replied. "My mother is very ill, and she's the one who's in the hospital."

"Oh, I'm sorry, hon." Fran walked over next to Shauna and placed her hand on her arm. "Would you like me to get you a sandwich or some meat loaf? It's really not as bad as it sounds." Grace watched her daughter look up at Fran and smile.

"I don't think so. At least not right now."

"Okay, hon. You let me know." Fran squeezed Shauna's arm and walked away.

Grace stared at her daughter and waited for her to say something. Shauna lowered her head, but she looked up at her mother.

"What?" she asked.

"What were you going to say before the food came?" Grace clenched her teeth. "Did you want to go eat at the hospital?"

"No." She lifted her head up. "My friends wanted me to go see a movie with them. But I told them I had to go sit at the hospital with you. I just thought I could eat a hot dog at the movie with them and come to the hospital later. I mean, it's not like Grandma knows we're even there." Shauna sighed. She folded her hands and placed them down in her lap.

"Grandma knows we're there, Shauna." Grace leaned forward and lowered her voice. "What if Grandma wakes up, and we're *not* there? What if the doctors need something, and I'm not there to give them the information? Or even worse, what if Grandma…"

Shauna stared down at the table and did not move. Her strawberry blond hair hung down in front of her face, covering her eyes. Grace looked away from Shauna. The young boy at the next table was staring back at her. His expression was now serious, and Grace saw his mother whisper something to him. He looked down at the table as he turned his head away.

"Grandma needs us right now, that's all I'm saying." Grace straightened her back and turned her whole body toward Shauna. She watched her daughter lift her head up.

As Shauna stared back at Grace, she squinted her eyes slightly. "Grandma has been asleep for five days. All we do is sit there and watch TV. I just wanted to go see a movie."

"And what about me?" Grace picked up half of her sandwich. "You're just going to leave me at the hospital all alone?"

Shauna stared at her mother. "Do you really need me there, Mom?"

"I…" Grace dropped her sandwich. White mayo covered the tips of her fingers, so she grabbed her napkin and wiped her hand clean. "If you're not going to go to the hospital with me, I think you should go home and clean the house."

Shauna continued to stare at her mother. "I cleaned the house last night, Mom. The kitchen was gross and there was cat hair all over the carpet."

"You can't expect me to do everything, Shauna. My mother is dying, and you want me to clean the house?"

"No, Mom. I just want to go see a movie." Shauna stared down at the table.

Grace looked up after a few seconds. She heard the young boy laugh, and she stared over at their table. His laugh was slow and loud, and it seemed to echo throughout the restaurant. Grace watched him as he stared at his mother and shook his head. *He's agreeing with everything she says*, Grace thought. The young boy continued to nod and let out short, loud laughs. He just nodded and laughed. Then nodded and laughed some more. He'd eat a French fry between laughs, and Grace was captivated by his exuberance.

When the young boy moved closer to his mother, Grace noticed two girls standing on the opposite side of the street. They were two of Shauna's friends from school, and she tried desperately to remember their names. Dozens of names came to mind, but she just couldn't think. Grace shook her head after she'd finally given up. She barely talked to her own friends now, so how would she ever be able to remember the names of Shauna's friends?

"What time does the movie start?"

"It's just down the street, and it starts in twenty minutes." Shauna pressed her lips together.

Grace reached down into her purse and pulled out a twenty dollar bill. "Do your friends want to do anything after the movie?" She waited and held the bill down in front of her.

"Actually, they wanted to go out to pizza, and then we were all gonna sleep over at Melinda's."

"But you don't have any clothes."

"I just told you, I bought an outfit this afternoon, and Melinda said I could borrow some of her pajamas."

Grace stared down at her plate. She handed Shauna the twenty. "Why don't you just tattoo *sucker* across my forehead."

Shauna grabbed the bill and sighed. "I've been at the hospital with you for five days, Mom. I just need some time away."

"I'd like some time for myself, too, Shauna." Grace stopped and lowered her voice. "I'm glad...I'm glad you're starting to have some fun. And I know this is an important time for you. But this is not fun for me. My mother is slowly slipping away from me, and there's nothing I can do. All I can do is sit there and wait."

"I know...and I'm sorry."

"So am I." Grace reached over and brushed Shauna's bangs out of her face, but she pulled away. "Go ahead, Shauna. Your friends are waiting for you."

Shauna sat up and looked out the window. Her friends were still standing across the street waiting. She turned to her mother with a guilty look and shoved the money in the pocket of her jeans as she stood up. "Thanks," she said quietly, leaving the table.

Grace watched her daughter walk away. Before Shauna opened the front door, Grace turned and saw the young boy watching Shauna's every move. He turned to his mother with a look of concern and pushed his empty plate to the opposite side of the table. He looked back over at Grace, but she turned her head away.

Grace watched Fran hand the young mother their check. The mother smiled at the waitress and pulled some money out of her purse. Fran walked past her with their dirty dishes. When Grace turned back toward their table, the mother had her prescription sunglasses on once again.

Grace watched as the young mother stood up from the table and pulled her purse strap up over her shoulder. She walked over to the door and then stopped and waited for her son. The boy still sat at the table, staring at Grace. He looked over at Shauna's empty chair and then stood up to join his mother. The young mother stood just outside with her back against the door, holding it open. The boy glanced up at Grace once as he left the table, and then stared down at the floor as he walked away. She looked away and stared at their empty table.

She heard the young boy say to his mother, "Wait." With a furrowed brow, the boy turned and stared at Grace with wide eyes. He opened his mouth and closed it quickly. His face turned red, and he looked pained; as if his words were stuck at the back of his throat, choking him. He stood silent for a second, took a quick gasp of breath, and said, "Goodbye."

Grace squinted her eyes and smiled. "Goodbye." Grace laughed as she watched the young boy's expression completely change. He smiled brightly, let out a short cough, and began to breathe again.

"I made that lady laugh, Mom," the boy said as he walked out past his mother.

"Good job, honey," the young mother replied. She too looked back at Grace and smiled. She placed her hand around her son's shoulders as they walked away.

Grace bent her head down and continued to laugh. "He made me laugh all right," she whispered to herself.

Grace finished her sandwich and even ate her pickle. She was hungrier than she had realized, and she sat back in her chair satisfied. Fran removed her plate and dropped off the check. Before she walked away, she looked down at Grace. "I hope everything works out okay with your mother." Grace looked up at the waitress and hoped she would smile at her again.

"Thanks."

Fran smiled.

"I appreciate that," she added.

When Grace walked out of the restaurant, she noticed the young mother and son standing in line at the movie theater down the street. The line was long for the afternoon show, and the mother and son stood at the side of the building with dozens of people in front of them. As Grace crossed the street, she looked toward the front of the line and saw Shauna standing there, laughing with her friends. Grace hoped Shauna would look up so she could wave at her, but the line began moving and Shauna and her friends walked closer to the entrance.

Grace looked down at her watch. It was 4:20. She had been away from the hospital for over an hour. Grace turned back to wave to Shauna, but she was no longer in sight. Grace glanced at her watch again. The car was just two blocks away. She turned from the theater and hurried down the street. Grace looked around. People were shopping. Couples were walking hand in hand, and a line of cars waited at the red light. Grace stopped. She took a deep breath and clenched her fists. She released her hands and clenched them again. Relaxing them again, she began walking slowly. As she moved forward, she rolled her shoulders back and stood up straight. She adjusted her purse strap and breathed deeply.

She thought of her daughter standing in line at the movie theater laughing with her friends, playing with her hair, and looking like a pretty young girl. Shauna had worked hard, suffered greatly for so many years, and become a different person. She had become Shauna, and the thought of her happiness made Grace smile. But all of that was quickly erased as she saw her car in front of her. She thought of her short drive to the hospital. She pictured the long hallways that led to her mother's room. And she remembered the image of her mother with tubes in her arms, wires strapped to her chest, and various machines all around her. "Keep moving," she whispered to herself, as she pushed forward and continued to walk toward it.

WORK AND LOVE IN YOUNG ADULTHOOD

GOOD HELP

Overwhelmed was the word that kept running through Linda's mind, even before she walked into Bellissima Bridal. With school, track practice, student government, babysitting, and working with her father and Nina Mary on putting together her *quinceañera,* she was pretty close to just going into some corner somewhere and crying. At times like this, Linda could vaguely remember what it was like to talk to her mother. Her mother with her slurred speech and her grand ambitions. Her mother, who was always half drunk and completely batshit crazy. Her mother, who had walked out on her when she was seven years old, left her and her father one night to go see an Oscar De La Hoya fight. She ran away from home with some strange man and never even called Linda or her father again.

La Loca, that's what the entire family called her mother now, and crazy is exactly how Linda felt as she stood in the middle of Bellissima Bridal. Her arms were crossed in front of her, and the tip of her fingernail was wedged between her teeth. Bellissima Bridal was not a very large store, but most everything inside was white. White wedding dresses lined the back walls; short, light-colored cocktail dresses hung from racks all around; wedding veils rested inside glass cabinets; and guest books, garter belts, white plume pens, and champagne glasses filled the display cases behind the counter. Linda stared at a headless mannequin standing in the corner. The white figure was wearing a white wedding dress with an incredibly short hemline. The mannequin's hands were empty, posed in front of it as if the plastic body had been caught by surprise. Probably surprised by the fact that everyone could see her white underwear, Linda thought. Linda took a deep breath and noticed her cousin, Diego, walking toward her.

"What up, *bitch*?" Diego said with a smirk.

"Que paso, *joto*?"

Diego gave his cousin a quick hug and then led her away from all of the white wedding gowns. "Ay, *tonta*, let's start over here." Diego walked forward and rested his hand on top of Linda's. "Don't worry. I'm here to help you. And we'll find you a dress." Linda followed and began to look around a bit more frantically.

"Now," Diego began again. "What I want you to do is sit down right here. You know Sophie, the owner, the one Mom calls the dark beauty, she's here, too. She and I will go and pull a few dresses for you and bring them out." He stopped Linda in front of two black sofas that stood in the center of the store. "I know what you need, and I know what you're looking for. So, just give us a few minutes. Sophie is finishing up with a mother and daughter in back."

"Excuse me." A woman with short blond hair emerged from the dressing rooms. She waved her hand in the air as she walked closer.

Diego broke away from Linda and turned around. Linda watched as Diego held two hands in front of him and tilted his head toward the woman. His short black hair shined brightly in the iridescent light, and his vintage half-frame glasses, black on top with silver wire on the bottom, made him look like a true fashion professional. Linda was impressed. Diego had started working in the bridal shop a little over a year ago. The entire family knew he was interested in fashion when he asked for a sewing machine for his tenth birthday. So, after a year of college, his mother, Linda's Nina Mary, put him in touch with Sophie, the store's owner. Now Diego was the head salesperson at Bellissima Bridal. The entire family was disappointed he would not complete his degree at the university, but his success here and his great interest in fashion was truly undeniable. To Linda, Diego was very special and unique. To the rest of the family, he was just plain different.

"Excuse me. Yeah...ah...hi...*sir*." The blond woman stopped a short distance in front of them. "My daughter wants to try on that other dress you just showed her." She looked at Diego. "I think my daughter wants to try a size eight."

"Size eight?" Diego said. "The last dress she tried on was a six."

"Well," the woman said, "just get her the dress, and we'll see how it fits." The woman turned her back and walked over to another rack of dresses. She flipped through them quickly and the hangers made a sharp noise as she dragged them along the metal rack.

"Have a seat," Diego said. "My mom should be here soon. So she, Sophie, and I will help you with all of this. Let's wait for her, and then we'll get started."

Linda moved closer to the two sofas and noticed an elderly woman sitting at the far end of one. The woman had short, white hair combed neatly into a bun at the back of her head. She wore a heavy polyester suit that was light gray, and she stared out the large display window facing the front entrance. Her hands were folded down in her lap, and she sat with her ankles crossed. The elderly woman didn't say a word or look at her. So, Linda sat down at the opposite end of the other sofa. She didn't want to block the elderly woman's view out the front window. Linda gazed at the woman's blank expression. She leaned forward and picked up one of the magazines fanned out on the coffee table in front of her. She opened the heavy magazine on her lap.

"Excuse me." Linda looked up and saw the blond woman standing at the other end of the coffee table. "Do you have this in a size eight?"

Linda turned her head from side and side and realized the woman was talking to her. She laughed at the woman. "Ah...I don't work here," Linda said, shaking her head. She focused on the magazine, but she could feel her throat begin to tighten as her head begin to throb. Overwhelmed, she thought to herself once again, and she focused on her deep breathing.

"You mean the only one working here now is that *little man*?" The blond woman draped the dress over one of her arms and looked around the store.

"*Little man*?" Linda replied, clamping her teeth tightly together. She purposely avoided looking back at the blond woman and instead stared at the elderly woman across from her. She exhaled slowly. "Like I said, I don't work here." The elderly woman continued to stare forward. "The owner of this shop is Sophie Marino. I think she's here right now, so if you ask the *little man*, whose name is Diego, I'm sure he can find her for you." Linda, moving her head as slowly as possible, turned and looked up at the blond woman. She gave the woman her best fake smile.

"Oh, Emily!" the blond woman said. She looked away from Linda at a young woman who'd emerged from the dressing room. The young woman wore a long white dress. The dress hung from her shoulders and the hem dragged on the ground all around her. Linda tilted her head and noticed the young woman was also wearing white pumps. She needs a size six petite, Linda thought.

Diego and Sophie stood directly behind the young woman and looked at her from head to toe. Sophie looked over at Linda, and Linda smiled and waved hello.

"Honey, that dress is beautiful. Isn't it, Mom?" The blond woman cupped her hands in front of her. She looked down at the elderly woman, who continued to stare out the front window. The blond woman moved over and sat down on the sofa. "Come over here and show Grandma your dress." She motioned for Emily to move in front of the coffee table. The blond woman placed her hand on the elderly woman's arm and leaned in closer.

"Mom, look at Emily's dress. Isn't it pretty?"

The grandmother turned and stared at Emily. "It is pretty," she said. "But it doesn't fit. It's too damn big." Her voice was quiet and calm as she stared down at the hem of the dress.

"Oh, they'll fix it," the blond woman said. She gripped the elderly woman's forearm and turned to Sophie and Diego. "How long will the alternations take?"

"We don't do alterations here," Sophie said as she stepped forward. "And I'm sorry, but that's the last dress we have in that style. I can give you the phone number of a seamstress we work with. Her shop is just down the street."

"You mean you're not a *seamstress*?" The blond woman sighed. She looked away from Sophie and stared over at Diego. "Are you a…? Do you sew? Can you fit the dress for us?"

"I'm a designer, and I can sew, but I don't do alterations. The woman we have does excellent work. So, we can give you her card, or we can start trying on some other dresses."

The blond woman shook her head and looked over at Linda. Linda rolled her eyes back down toward her magazine. "Do you really love that dress, honey?" the blond woman asked her daughter.

"Yes," Emily said. "The cotillion is in three weeks, Mom, and I have to have a white dress."

The mother held up her hand. "Then we'll get it fixed, honey. Don't worry." She looked away from Emily and stared over at the elderly woman. Emily picked up the front of the dress and walked back toward the dressing rooms. Sophie and Diego followed.

"I can't believe *they* don't do alterations here." The mother sat up straight on the sofa and leaned away from the grandmother. Linda could tell that she was staring over at her, probably looking for some kind of sympathy, but Linda continued to study one of the pictures in the magazine. "Now I have to call this *other woman* and go someplace else for fittings. I just can't believe that *one of them* can't do the alterations. I mean, why do *people like that* work here if they can't do the alternations themselves?" The mother looked over at the grandmother, who was shaking her head in agreement. She added, "You just can't find *good help* these days."

Linda looked over at the two women and heard the bell that hung from the front door ring. She watched the grandmother look over at the door and wondered if she would regain her blank expression and begin staring out the front window again. The grandmother patted her daughter's leg and tilted her head closer. "That reminds me," the grandmother said. "I have to hire a new maid sometime this week." Her voice was just above a whisper, but Linda could hear every word. The mother looked over her shoulder toward the front of the store.

"What happened to your maid?" the blond woman asked.

"She chipped some of my crystal while she was dusting, and I just discovered it last week. I had to let her go." Both women stared at the front door.

Linda turned her head to see who had just walked in. An older woman with dark hair stood just inside the door. She wore a blue cotton dress covered with large, embroidered flowers. A heavy purse hung from one arm, and she held on to the top of a black wooden cane with her other hand. She steadied herself on the cane and looked around the store.

Linda smiled and held her hand up. "Nina!" she shouted and waved. She stood up from the sofa and placed the magazine back on the table. Her Nina Mary walked over and met her at one end of the black sofas.

"Ay, my Linda, I'm so sorry I'm late," she said. Linda held out her arms and placed them around her aunt.

"Thank you for coming, Nina." Linda hugged her tightly and stepped back. She slipped her arm around her Nina's elbow, and they walked together back to her end of the sofa. When they sat down, Nina Mary let go of her cane and held on to Linda's hand.

"Does my Diego have a nice dress for you to try on?" Nina Mary rested her purse at her side.

"He says he has several he wants me to take a look at."

"Do you like any of them?"

Linda looked over at the two women to see if they were staring back at her. The grandmother stared blankly out the front window again, and the mother was turned around in the sofa, looking back toward the dressing rooms.

"I haven't seen any of the dresses yet. We wanted to wait for you. We'll just have to decide on one together."

"*Mijita*," Nina Mary said, looking down at their hands. "I want to buy this dress for you."

"Nina, I can…"

"No. No. I will take care of it. Your father has so much to worry about. And besides, your *quinceañera* only comes once in your life. And I want it to be beautiful." Nina Mary lifted her hand and brushed her thumb against Linda's cheek.

"All right," Linda replied. The grandmother was now

staring down at the floor. Her eyes were empty and her folded hands shook slightly. The mother now stood outside of the dressing area next to Emily. Sophie walked around them and held the white gown up high in front of her.

"Hi, Doctora Enriquez," Sophie said. She placed the gown over her bended forearm, leaned down, and gave Nina Mary a kiss on the cheek.

"Ay, Sophia, my beautiful *Italiana*," Nina Mary said, shaking her hand in front of her face. "Do you have some pretty dresses for my Linda?"

"Yes, we have several we want her to look at, and we'll bring them out shortly." Sophie held Nina Mary's hand. "Just let me ring up this sale, and then I'm all yours." Sophie walked over to the register where Diego was already handing the mother the business card of their favorite seamstress.

"Did you have any problems getting away from school today?" Linda asked as she watched Diego look over and wave hello to his mother. Nina Mary waved back.

"No, *mijita*. I let my class go early today and told my students to catch up on their reading." Nina Mary looked over at the grandmother, who was still sitting silently on the opposite sofa. The elderly woman did not look back. She just stared down at the ground.

"What are you having your students read now?" Linda said in a slightly louder voice.

"Poetry," Nina Mary said. "My undergraduates love poetry, so I'm having them read some Sor Juana Ines de la Cruz. Maybe they'll learn something about Mexican women." Linda smiled.

At the register, Emily held the white dress up in front of her. It was now covered with clear plastic, and Emily rustled the bag loudly as she tried to keep it up off the floor. The mother walked back over and sat down on the sofa next to the grandmother. She placed her hand on the grandmother's shoulder and said, "We're all done, Mom. It's time to go."

"Oh," the grandmother said. "Okay. I'm ready." She pushed herself forward on the sofa. The mother bent down and held on to the grandmother's arm. She helped the elderly woman to her feet and then turned away. She walked over to Emily and took the clear garment bag away from her daughter.

"You're letting it drag on the ground. How about we get that *other woman* to fix it before you start destroying it. Mom, we're leaving!" she added as she trailed her daughter out of the store.

The grandmother stood quietly in front of the sofa. She looked over at Linda and Nina Mary and smiled. "I don't move as quickly as I used to," she said.

"I know," Nina Mary replied. "Takes me fifteen minutes to just get out of the car."

The grandmother laughed.

"Go help her, *mijita*." Nina Mary motioned for Linda to go over and assist the grandmother. Linda sprang to her feet. She placed one hand carefully behind the grandmother's back and guided the elderly woman out from behind the coffee table. The grandmother squeezed Linda's arm when they had made their way to the front of the store.

"I can take it from here, honey. But thank you. I appreciate your help." The grandmother slipped her arm out of Linda's and stared out the front door. She continued to walk slowly toward the door with Linda walking slightly behind her. Linda moved forward cautiously with both hands held out in front of her. Diego stepped around them and opened the front door. The grandmother turned back toward Linda and Nina Mary. "They bring me all this way and then forget me in the store.

How do you like that?" She slapped her hands together and laughed.

"And you even helped them pick out such a pretty dress," Diego said, as he stood with the open door behind his back and waited for her to pass.

"Oh, they didn't need my help." She moved closer to Diego. "I used to sew, but now my hands are so bad I can't even help them with that."

Linda walked closely behind the elderly woman. "Well, I think you helped out a lot," Linda said to the grandmother's back. "And you know what they say?"

"What's that?" the grandmother asked. She looked past Diego out into the parking lot. "I'm coming. I'm coming!" she yelled and stepped out of the store.

Linda watched the elderly woman as she struggled to move faster. She looked back at her Nina Mary, who sat with her hands resting on the top of her cane. She then moved past Diego, to just outside the front door, and yelled to the grandmother, "You know what they say! *Good help* is hard to find these days!"

Linda stopped cold when the young blond woman turned her head and fixed her eyes on Linda. Her forehead began to crinkle like a discarded tissue, and she continued to stare forward with her lips pursed tightly together. The young mother looked as if anger and pain were shooting out of her, and it was all pointed in Linda's direction. She stared coldly at Linda, and Linda calmly stared back at her.

"Wow," Diego said after a few seconds of complete silence. "You are getting to be such a *little bitch*."

Linda burst out laughing. She couldn't help herself. She turned around and realized she had finally unclenched her teeth and that her head felt a lot lighter. She took a deep breath, stared back at Diego, and said, "Shut up, *joto*." She stepped closer to him, smiled brightly, and then added, "Now, *little man*, be a *doll* and help me find a fabulous dress for my *quinceañera*?"

"Right this way," Diego said as he smiled at his cousin, took her by the hand, and helped her back into the store.

Rustin Baines

His name was Rustin Baines, which I always thought was really cool until I found out that it was his working name. Rustin was this beautiful twenty-year-old man who'd show up at the restaurant regularly. He had short blond hair that he spiked up in front, with dark brown eyes and clear white skin that looked flawless. It wasn't until months later I found out Rustin wore a light foundation to make his skin look so healthy, and he sometimes shaved his face twice to make his skin look as clean as possible.

But when he walked into the restaurant, people turned and looked at him. He was an interesting mixture of masculine and feminine, but with his broad shoulders and large hands, he looked like a strong and sophisticated gay man. And he was always put together so perfectly: polished shoes, tailored pants, pressed shirt, and the perfect tie.

Rustin was quiet and smart, and he'd always acknowledge me with a slight nod of his head. He'd then stand silently alone in front of the large window that faced the busy street outside. He'd wait for his date to meet him. And he knew I'd always give him the best table in the house. Rustin liked being seen, and I guess it helped him find richer and more sophisticated boyfriends.

At the time, I was a host in a small Italian restaurant in Tucson. We were the place to be for young professionals who liked to eat osso buco or braciola and drink shitty pink wine, either Italian rosé or California white zinfandel. I became the restaurant's evening host in 1986 at the age of nineteen, and although I had no idea how to run the floor of one of the busiest restaurants in town, I could fake it like no one else I knew. No one, that is, except for Rustin Baines.

I was finishing up my bachelor's degree in chemistry at the University of Arizona. As the first member of my large Mexican-American family to go to college, I worked all the time. I did everything I could to complete my degree as quickly as possible. I took a full course load during the day and ran the front of the restaurant at night. I rarely ever saw my family, which was okay, because as a closeted young gay man, I was still trying to find my way out. So, I only saw my mother and father on holidays, and I only talked about school and work. No one in my family could afford to come and eat at the restaurant, and no one would ever dare set foot on campus, so I led a life that was sheltered, protected, and lonely.

I first noticed Rustin when he started coming into the restaurant regularly with a man named Terry McQuirk. Terry was, of course, an older man with frizzy gray hair. He always wore loose fitting V-neck sweaters that were either cream colored or yellow, with matching pants, and at least two or three thin gold chains around his neck. He was an old gay stereotype, or as our day manager would call him, he was one of the *Boys in the Band*.

I only knew Terry had money based on his bright red convertible. He would always make a point to drive slowly past the big window at the front of the restaurant before coming in for dinner. I always thought it was his way of checking to see if Rustin was waiting for him, but I later came to realize he was also making sure I saw him in his expensive convertible. Terry was always happy to see me and was very respectful. He made his Saturday reservations under the names Terry McQuirk with Rustin Baines, because he wanted me to know both of them would be joining us for dinner. Terry was a sweet old guy, and he always looked like he wanted to kiss Rustin the minute he walked into the restaurant. But, of course, he never did. He would sometimes try to hold Rustin's hand as they'd walk over and check in with me at the host's desk, but Rustin would pull away and ask to be seated.

After seeing the two of them together every Saturday night for at least six months, Terry was gone. I don't know what happened to him, and I never asked Rustin. Rustin and I rarely ever exchanged words. He was there to meet his dates, and I was there to provide him with the best table in the house. For the next few Saturdays, Rustin showed up with a different older man. He would have a reservation on our busy Saturday nights, but it would always be under the name of his date.

And it was up to me to juggle the reservations and provide Rustin with the nicest table. I don't know how I did it, but I'd always put him in the best seat in the house. He'd get the best lighting in the center of the restaurant, with his back to the wall, facing out into the dining room where everyone who entered the restaurant could see him and he could see each and every one of them. It was Rustin's way of testing me to see if I would take care of him or let him down. And I moved heaven and hell to make him happy and get his ass into the perfect seat.

When I had started my second year at the restaurant, Rustin showed up one evening with Dr. James Blakely. And when I saw the way Rustin looked at his new date, I knew something had changed in the way Rustin was playing his game. Dr. Blakely was a general surgeon with his own practice in town. He must have been about fifty-five years old at the time, and he was a tall, thick man with short gray hair and dark blue eyes. Friendly and professional are the words I would use to describe Dr. Blakely. The moment he walked into the restaurant, before he noticed Rustin waiting for him by the front window, he held out his hand to me and asked me my name.

"I'm Diego Martinez."

"Hi. Nice to meet you." He shook my hand and looked me right in the eyes. "I'm Dr. James Blakely. I have a seven o'clock reservation. I'm meeting someone."

"James," Rustin said, stepping toward us.

"Yes, Dr. Blakely. I have your table ready for you."

"Thanks." Dr. Blakely never looked over at Rustin. He just shot him a quick smile and moved past me to look into the dining room. "Can we get a table in the back room?"

"Sure," I replied and asked one of the waiters to go and check on a table for me. "It'll just be one second." I took my place behind the host's station again and tried to give the two of them some privacy.

"So, James, how are you?" Rustin asked.

"I'm fine. How are you?" Again, he did not look at Rustin, just back into the dining room. I watched Rustin move closer to him, and I could see how much he wanted to reach out and take Dr. Blakely's hand. But, of course, he never did.

Turning my head away, I then heard Dr. Blakely ask, "So, Diego, are you from Tucson?"

Gritting my teeth, not wanting to get involved, I replied, "Yes. I'm a native. Born and raised."

"Wow, that's pretty rare around here. Most people come from somewhere else."

The whole time Dr. Blakely spoke, I watched Rustin

staring blankly at Dr. Blakely's hand. I couldn't tell if he was happy or sad; just mesmerized by the doctor's right hand. And I could sense how much Rustin wanted to reach out and touch him.

Trying to get my attention again, Dr. Blakely asked, "Diego, do you go to U of A?"

"Yeah. I'm a senior, majoring in chemistry."

"So, what do you wanna do with a degree in chemistry?"

"I'm also pre-med. And I'm applying to medical school this year."

"Wow. Have you completed all your pre-med courses?"

"Yeah. Finished Organic Chemistry last semester."

"You know O-Chem separates the men from the boys. Did you do well?"

"Yeah. I got an A. I get As in all of my classes." I didn't mean to say that. It just slipped right out of me. And Rustin turned and shot me the coldest stare I've ever seen.

"That's great. Do you want to go to med school here in Tucson?"

"Yes," I said. "I want to stay close to family and friends."

Just then the waiter returned. "Your table is all set and ready," he said, respectfully holding his hands behind his back.

"Great," I replied. Turning away from Dr. Blakely, I handed the waiter two menus. "Would you please take them to their table? Enjoy your meal," I added as I watched them walk away. An hour later, I found myself peeking into the back room to see how Rustin was getting along. From what I could tell, he and Dr. Blakely were having a lively conversation over a nice bottle of red wine and two half-eaten portions of the veal special. Rustin looked happy in his dark corner of the room, and I could hear his laughter throughout the restaurant for the first time.

Rustin returned to the restaurant for the next two months on Saturday evenings with Dr. Blakely. True to form, he continued his routine of nodding to me and taking his place by the front window. When Dr. Blakely would arrive, usually five minutes later, he'd ask me twenty questions before even acknowledging his date.

For the first few weeks, Dr. Blakely anxiously shook my hand and asked me about my applications to medical school. He even offered me advice on how to improve my personal statement. Eventually, his questions focused on my clinical experience, and he advised me on how much volunteer time I needed in a hospital or clinic to make my application more competitive. And finally his questions focused on my experience shadowing any physicians. The good doctor even offered to have me observe him during some routine surgeries. He said I could borrow some of his scrubs. I'd just have to meet him in the men's locker room of the hospital, and we could change there together. While I did enjoy Dr. Blakely's expertise and attention, I soon began to realize how abusive it was becoming to Rustin.

As Dr. Blakely would excitedly ask me questions and occupy my attention while the entire restaurant filled up on a Saturday evening, he'd also make little side comments about Rustin:

"Wow, with your experience, Diego, you should sail right into med school. Rustin here can't even add an eighteen percent tip to the check at the end of the evening."

Or:

"You have a great future in front of you, Diego. I think it's so great that you're smart and motivated, and have so much more going for you than your handsome face."

And eventually it all ended with:

"God, and you've paid all of your own tuition in college.

Rustin would have to spend a lot of nights on his back to raise that kind of money."

With that last comment, I had had enough. In the midst of all of this, I had somehow become involved in some sort of fucked-up madonna/whore scenario. And as a young gay Latino who was just waiting to burst out of the closet, I did not want to be the madonna.

That's why I paid less and less attention to Rustin and Dr. Blakely as I worked toward my last day at the restaurant when I was finally able to say goodbye to that life and begin my new life in medical school.

I arranged for my final night at the restaurant to be a Saturday. And like every Saturday for the past nine or ten weeks, Rustin and Dr. Blakely had a reservation for seven o'clock.

When Rustin walked in that night, I was standing at the bar. My replacement, Tracy, who I was training to take over as hostess, was standing at the host's station. Rustin nodded to her and again waited by the front window. He looked back at her and then over at me before pointing his index finger and curling it back toward him several times, beckoning me over.

"Diego," he said.

"Rustin."

"Who's the new girl?"

"This is Tracy. She will be taking over for me in the evenings." I could hear Tracy say "Hi" in the background, but neither one of us turned around to acknowledge her.

"Are you leaving us?"

"Yes. I am going to medical school."

I could hear Dr. Blakely behind us.

"Hello," he said to Tracy. "I'm Dr. James Blakely. I have a reservation for seven o'clock."

"Yes, Dr. Blakely. I have your table ready for you."

"Tracy," I said, waiting for her to look back at me. "I'll take them to their table. Would you check with the kitchen and make sure they know how many reservations we have for this evening?"

Tracy smiled and walked back into the dining room.

"James," Rustin began. "Diego here is going away to medical school, and he is training Tracy as his replacement. Isn't that nice?"

"Tonight is my last night."

"Congratulations," Dr. Blakely said, taking my hand and shaking it wildly. Still holding on to my hand and moving closer toward me, he added, "So, you got into medical school. That's great news. What school will you be attending?"

"It's called Pomona. It's a small osteopathic school in California."

"I thought you wanted to stay here and go to med school at U of A."

"U of A didn't accept me."

"Why not? Seems like you were a perfect candidate."

"I guess they had a problem with my application."

Dr. Blakely finally let go of my hand. He lowered his eyebrows and looked away. "You know. I know the Director of Admissions there. I could call her and see what happened. I'm sure there must have been some kind of mix-up or something."

"Oh, no." I looked over at Rustin, who was staring back at me. "There was no mix-up." I looked down at the ground and thought about walking away or saying what I had to say. "There was a problem with my application." I looked back at Rustin and stared into his eyes the whole time I spoke. "U of A does a background check on all applicants who indicate they've spent some time in jail. Most medical schools do. You see..." I stopped and watched Rustin tilt his head toward me.

"U of A found out I have a criminal record. For some stupid stuff I did when I was younger. U of A doesn't forgive you for your past mistakes, but thankfully, Pomona does. If you can afford to pay their tuition. So, I'm going there."

"I see," Dr. Blakely moaned.

Rustin squinted his eyes, as if he didn't understand what I was saying.

I turned and saw Tracy standing at the bar. I motioned for her to come back over and join us.

"I'm sorry, Tracy," I said. "But would you show Rustin and Dr. Blakely to their table." I moved behind the host's desk and checked the reservation book. "Take them to table 38." I looked back at Rustin. "That's the one booth in the center of the restaurant under the lights, with the large DeGrazia painting behind it."

"Sure. Right this way."

When Tracy returned, I told her I needed to go outside and get some fresh air.

As I stood on the other side of the large window at the front of the restaurant, I heard the door open and saw Rustin Baines standing next to me.

"Hey," he said.

"Hey."

We stood in silence for a few seconds, staring out into the busy street in front of us.

"I'm sorry you're leaving," he said.

"Yeah. Well, I need to move beyond this fucking restaurant."

"Yeah." He paused. "Become a doctor."

"Yeah."

After a few more seconds of silence, he asked, "Did you really not get into U of A's med school?"

I looked over at him and smiled. "Why? You don't believe me?"

"No. I don't fucking believe you."

"Well, you're right. I start at U of A in August. I did get in. And I'm gonna stay in Tucson."

"So, what? You were bullshitting us with that criminal record stuff?"

"Yeah. I was. And do you understand why?"

"Cuz James is a giant asshole, and you wanted to stop impressing him."

"Kinda. Well, that's part of it. Seems the more I impress him, the more he's an asshole to you."

"Do you think you're protecting me, Diego Martinez?"

"No." I stopped and laughed. "I'm just working on my own image. Or the image I have of myself. So, fuck Dr. James Blakely. I guess he'll eventually find out I'm still in town, at U of A, but I don't give two shits about what he thinks of me. And how hard he tries to help me."

"Yeah." Rustin laughed. "All the while he's pushing your hand toward his crotch." We both laughed. "Ya know he's just trying to be nice."

"Whatever."

"You are bent, Diego Martinez."

"And that means so much coming from you, Rustin Baines."

He laughed, turned, and walked over to the front door of the restaurant. Before he opened the door, he stopped and added, "We should hang out sometime."

I smiled, feeling like I'd just won the grand prize.

"Sure." Before I could stop myself, I said, "But I don't know if I can afford you."

Rustin smiled and opened the door. "Take me out for

a drink tonight, and we'll discuss it. I'll be free at ten." But before heading inside, he leaned against the open door and said, "And ya know, Diego Martinez…" He pointed his finger in the air, and then over at me. "I am my own boss. And for you, it'll always be free."

Sex, Love, and Intellectual Property

Mrs. Brickman was the woman in his story, with her light gray hair, wide-brimmed hat, bright yellow blouse, royal blue cotton pants, and her grabber tool. When I realized it was her, I stopped in the middle of the road.

She held a long, white aluminum tool with dark gray jaws that clicked together at the bottom. The device was engineered to tightly grab on to small items without Mrs. Brickman having to bend over or reach down into the gravel of her front yard. With her grabber tool, Mrs. Brickman was methodically clearing away the long yellow seed pods that fell from her mesquite tree. With a black bucket at her side, she stood in one position and picked up one seed pod after the other. Individually she carefully placed them into her plastic bucket and used the tool to reach back down for another.

Without bending or turning, she meticulously worked her way through a small section of the yard. One section of the gravel was completely clean. It appeared as if she had cleared away a fourth of the seed pods that covered the ground underneath the tree. I had no idea how long it had taken her, but I was amazed at how patiently she went about her work.

Mrs. Brickman was a neighbor. She lived about a block away from my condo. I had only met her once, over five years ago at a neighborhood watch meeting. A few of the houses in our neighborhood had been robbed, and we all came together to see what we could do. Back then Mrs. Brickman was quiet, sweet, and very old. But now she was even older; probably in her early nineties. And she seemed to be the kind of woman who wanted to stay active and keep her mind as sharp as possible.

I had never seen her out in her front yard before, clearing away the yellow seed pods with her long grabber tool, but Tom had used her, or carefully described this image of her, in one of his short stories. He'd written it over five years ago, and it stood out in his collection, which needs to find a publisher but lies dormant on my dining room table in a large manila envelope.

Tom Horne worked for the University of Arizona when I met him ten years ago. He was cerebral, introverted, and a hell of a lot of fun. He looked like the actor Edward Norton in the film *American History X*. Not as young and thin and in shape, but pretty damn close. We met at an outreach event sponsored by Tom's job. Tom was an admissions counselor at U of A, and the event included high school students from South Tucson.

At the time, I was a new employee in U of A's College of Medicine, and I had my own browsing table at the event. I spoke to students and parents about careers in the health professions and about our health-related majors at U of A. Tom was essentially in charge of the event, and I noticed him looking at me the moment I set up my table. He never introduced himself. I just remember him coming over and asking me how everything was going. We talked for less than a minute and before he left, he put his hand on my right shoulder, squeezed it slightly, and walked away.

I had to leave my table unattended and find the closest

bathroom. I wiped my face down with cold water. I was anxious and excited, and I had never experienced anything like that before. When he put his hand on me, I saw our future together. I knew it wouldn't be a long-term relationship. It would be shallow and sexual. And I knew we'd never buy his and his matching BMWs and settle down in the suburbs of southern Arizona. All I knew was I wanted to move forward with whatever was going to happen between us. And then see where I was in life.

After seeing each other again at various university events, Tom asked me out. We went to a house party for one of his friend's birthdays, but we left early. We ended up at the gay bar on 4th Ave. It was still early in the evening, and we were the only couple sitting together at the outside bar on the back patio.

Tom was talkative but cautious. I could tell he wanted to touch me or reach out and hold my hand, but he kept leaning back in his chair and sitting on his right hand. At the time, I was just starting my doctoral work in the College of Education. I was a part-time student at night and worked full-time during the day in the College of Medicine. Tom, on the other hand, had just finished his MFA in Creative Writing. He had taught at the university while working on his degree but now worked full-time as an admissions counselor. He liked working with students and kept an early work schedule so he could write well into the evenings.

We both ordered a beer, and I turned my chair toward him. "So, are you working on anything right now? A novel or play? I'm not sure what you write."

"I'm not working on anything right now. After three years in the MFA program, I'm taking a short break from writing."

We sat in silence for a few seconds before Tom let out a short laugh.

"You know, when I met you, I couldn't figure out if you were gay or not."

"Well, it's hard to be obviously gay at a work event."

"Yeah." He let out another odd little laugh. "I don't think it was until the third or fourth time I saw you that I decided you might actually be gay and possibly interested in me."

"That first time I met you, I knew you were gay."

"But you? You're a hard person to read. I mean, you're what I'd call stoic."

"Stoic?"

"Yeah."

"I've been called a lot of things. But I've never been called stoic."

"I don't mean it as an insult."

"And I'm not taking it as one."

"You're very in charge of your own little world."

"I wouldn't call my world little, but I do like things done in a certain way. Especially when it comes to work. And you've really only seen me in work mode."

"That's why I wanted to ask you out. To get to know you better."

"What about you? You, on the other hand, you seem…I don't know. I'd like to think of one word to describe you, but it's just not coming."

Tom smiled. "So, use more than one word."

"You seem like you're very in tune with your own observations. You know what you see, and you like to name it or even label it."

"I'm a writer. I love language."

"Yeah, but I'm an educator. I love language, too, but I don't like labels."

"So what? You want to look deeper?"

"I want to look at more than just what's on the surface."

We sat in silence again. Tom looked into my eyes and didn't break away.

"Let's get out of here," he said.

"Okay. Let's go."

That night we went to my place. I live in a small two-bedroom condo close to the university. It's the kind of place where I should have a roommate, but I don't. Tom took off my clothes, and I took off his. We moved slowly at first but then began to kiss each other deeper and deeper. But the moment I felt myself begin to relax, the moment I began to let go and allow myself to move closer to him, he pulled away.

He made some feeble excuse, grabbed his stuff, and left my bedroom. I could hear him in the hallway, pulling on his clothes, but I just lay there in shock. When I heard the front door close behind him, I knew I was exactly where I expected to be the moment I met him. Alone. Alone, lonely, and frustrated.

Tom sent me a gutless email a few days later. I remember the title of the email was "Living Rooms." Tom said he wasn't ready for where we were going that night, and we should begin a relationship by getting to know each other and staying in the living room. I, on the other hand, had no problem with where we were headed or what we were doing. If anything, I wanted to get the sex out of the way to see if the relationship had a future or if I was just wasting my time.

Our work lives brought us together a couple more times within the next few months. Before I knew it, Tom was talking and flirting with me as if nothing had ever happened. But I wanted to have sex. So, I asked him out to dinner. I made some smart-ass comment about how we would eat a nice meal, and that the evening would only end up in the living room. But that was not the case. We did have a nice meal at one of my favorite restaurants, and by the end of the evening we were back in my bedroom. Tom was naked in my bed, and I was on top of him. I told him there was no way he was running away from me that night.

The sex was average at first—somewhat mechanical and very routine. When we were done, Tom always left in a rush or hurried me out of his apartment. And for me, that was okay. I was having sex with a man I really wanted to have sex with, and it was nice. But before we knew it, we were really getting to know each other, both on an intellectual and a physical level. By the time I met Tom's two best friends, and we were all hanging out together and having fun, sex with Tom had become fantastic.

We were members of a small group of friends. That's how things operated for me and Tom. There were Tom's two best friends, who we saw often, and eventually we added my best friend and a few other friends from the gay bars. But we were always together with friends in a small group. Being social came easy to Tom. Being liked by others also became important to Tom. He often did not like being alone with me; having a one-on-one conversation for him was rather boring. Possibly not enough stimulation or attention.

While we did have amazing sex, and I began to feel an incredible level of intimacy with him, it was always short lived. Our time alone, together alone, was always finite. It always came to a quick ending. So, we never went away together. We never slept past eight in the morning if we spent the night at each other's place, and we never talked about our feelings or a future together.

That's why one party came as such a shock to me. We were celebrating one of our friends' birthday at a pool party.

Tom and I had been drinking a lot of beer and ended up alone together in the Jacuzzi. If I had thought about it, I should have known this conversation was coming. But I never allowed myself to think about a future with Tom.

"You know it's been two years." Tom put down his beer and stood facing me in the middle of the Jacuzzi.

"Two years since that first night and the 'Living Rooms' email?"

"Yeah, I guess."

"I didn't think I'd ever see you again after that night."

"Well, two years and you haven't been able to get rid of me."

"I never wanted to get rid of you in the first place."

"You've always been really patient with me. I like that about you."

"I'm a teacher. If I see a challenge, I always figure out a way to overcome it."

"As a writer, I guess I always want to deconstruct it," he said.

"Or label it. Call it what it is."

"Yeah, I guess."

"Why didn't you just move on after that night and leave me alone? I mean, two years ago? I always knew you didn't want to go where we were headed."

"I wanted to get to know you," he said.

"So, do you think you know me now?"

"I know I love you."

And there we were. With those words. The words I'd wanted to hear. Tom was the first man in my openly gay life to tell me he loved me. My first reaction was one of anger. What the fuck did he want from me? I knew he wanted me to open up to him even more, let down my guard so he could pull away from me again. I was dumbfounded, and I let my homosexual self get the best of me. I stopped listening to my intuition and just let myself go.

"I love you, too."

We looked around. We were alone in the Jacuzzi at our friend's apartment complex, and although we wanted to grab a hold of each other, we didn't. We just picked up our beers and moved to a couple of lounge chairs close by. Tom told me he loved me two or three more times and talked about our future together. He said he wanted to keep working at the university, eventually buy a house and raise a few kids. I just sat and listened. I knew once I joined into the conversation, it would all change. It would not become real, and he would pull away and break my heart. So, I listened for as long as I could and then said, "I think it's time you let me read some of your stories."

"Yeah," he said. His eyes lost focus, and he looked away.

"I know your master's thesis is in the library, and I can read it any time I want to. But I'd really like to read your copy or anything else you want to share with me."

"Yeah?"

"Is that okay? Do you want me to read your work?"

"Yes. I…I do. It's just that I've been working on this one story, and I don't know if I'm ready to share it."

"I'd still like to read what you wrote in grad school. I know your thesis is a collection of about ten stories, so I'd really like to read that."

"How do you know about my thesis?"

"I did look at it in the library one day. But I didn't read it. I wanted to wait and see if you'd give me a copy."

"Yeah. I have my copy. I'll give it to you tonight when we get home. Or maybe share with you the one story I've been working on. It's not in my thesis."

When we got back to his place that night, we had sex all over his apartment. I remember starting off on the coffee table and ending up in the shower. At that moment, he was mine, and I felt I truly belonged to him. Every time I looked into his eyes, I told him that I loved him. I held him as close as I possibly could, and he let me. By the end of the evening, the word love kept flowing out of me and I could not control myself.

I knew I should stop. I knew I should pace myself, slow my feelings down a bit, but I also felt as if I had won. I had waited. I had listened to that little voice inside me that said to wait for him to tell you he loves you first. Wait for him to fall in love with you, and then you can allow yourself to tell him. Tell him what you've felt the moment you first met him. Tell him you love him, and you'd do anything to be with him.

As I left Tom's apartment that next morning, he asked me to wait as he printed out a fresh copy of the story he'd been working on. He shared with me the story he'd just completed and was now just beginning to circulate for publication. The story he called "A Methodical Cleaning."

As I sat and read Tom's short story, I wondered if I would come to understand him better; if we'd grow closer now that I was reading his work and had a better understanding of what he did and who he was. I didn't know if the story would provide insight into Tom's psyche or how he thought about life. But I knew a great part of him was in that story, and I wanted to understand it and him as much as possible.

"A Methodical Cleaning" was the story of a woman who was at the end of her life. The main character, Helen, would clean her front yard with her long grabber tool. She'd use the tool to pick up the yellow seed pods that fell from her mesquite tree. Then, one by one, she'd place the pods in her black bucket. As she did so, Helen made plans for her funeral. She also planned for what would happen to all of her possessions when she was gone. Helen was not suicidal, and she was not dying of any disease. She was not a tragic figure in any sense, but a strong character who knew what she wanted and focused on her own peace of mind. She knew her life was coming to an end, and she wanted to put everything in order before she actually left this world. So, Helen spent most of the story figuring out who in her life would take care of her estate after she was gone. She worked her way through the important people in her life and ended up leaving everything to her young niece, who was the only member of her family smart enough to carry out her final plans and caring enough to respect her final wishes.

I found Tom's writing to be plain and beautiful. While Helen was a simple character, I found the metaphor of her cleaning her front yard awe-inspiring. When I had finished the story, I read it again, and I knew I had become even closer to Tom. That idea scared me, but I pushed through those feelings and called him and told him I loved him.

I asked Tom for the rest of his stories, but he kept putting me off. We were always on our way to spend time with friends, or we were off to yet other work event, and he never shared another story with me. Eventually, Tom stopped saying he loved me, and we stopped having sex. While I tried to coax him into saying those words after I had said them to him so many times, they never came again. After visualizing a future of fighting and more and more frustration, I told Tom we should stop seeing each other. He had no problem with that. I had gathered a few of his things in a small pile and placed my copy of his short story at the bottom. The pile sat on my coffee table in front of him as he agreed to end our relationship. Then, after a moment of silence, he picked up his stuff, and he was gone.

Six months later, I found out Tom had married an older man. They had met, fallen in love, and gotten married in Vermont, where gay marriage had just been legalized. It was awful and painful, and I kept wondering why it hadn't been me. My main frustration with my relationship with Tom was that I should have known better. Every ounce of my being at that time told me not to fall in love with him. Not to move too quickly and open myself up to someone new. And to listen to that little voice in my head that told me that he would eventually break my heart. And I was right.

If I had listened to my intuition, which I often do, I would not have gone through that experience. I would not have been left wondering why he could not commit himself to me, and why I wasn't the one traveling to Vermont to marry a man who loved me. I was also left wondering if Tom really loved me and if two men could really love each other enough to make a lasting commitment.

After three more years, I received a phone call that yet again changed my life. Tom's best friend, who I hadn't spoken to in forever, called me to tell me Tom had been killed by a drunk driver. Tom was driving home by himself from a university event and was rear-ended by a drunk driver. His car was pushed into oncoming traffic, and he was hit by another car head-on. He lived for twenty-four hours after the accident but died due to severe head trauma. Tom was thirty-seven years old.

I thought that was the end of my story with Tom Horne. While I grieved silently for a relationship that had ended over five years ago, I woke up one morning to see Tom's best friend standing at my front door. In his hands was a copy of Tom's last will and testament along with a large manila envelope filled with Tom's short stories. While Tom had left all of his possessions and his life insurance money to his husband, he left his stories, his intellectual property, to me. Inside the manila envelope were eleven short stories—the ten stories that made up his master's thesis and his final short story, "A Methodical Cleaning."

I was one of the people in his life who would take care of the things that mattered to him, even after he left this world. I can't even begin to explain why Tom wouldn't leave these stories to his husband. But then again, I don't know his husband. And I can't even imagine when Tom wrote his will, but I am the one he knew he could trust with his short stories. I know now that Tom loved me, and he trusted me enough to continue his quest. I am now the one who will find a place to publish his collection and keep his stories alive. From my time with Tom, I have come to follow several of the literary magazines that he loved, and I know where he would have wanted to publish his work. As I read more and more of his stories, I know they are a big part of his life and something he wanted to continue to share.

I've already begun to circulate his story, "A Methodical Cleaning." I know it'll take some time, but I'll keep trying to publish some of his individual short stories, and then the entire collection as a book. I see this as my challenge now, and it's a challenge I know I can meet. And when I do publish "A Methodical Cleaning," I'll walk over and share it with my neighbor, Mrs. Brickman. I'll share with her his story of an older woman who used a grabber tool to help plan the final details of her long life. And share with her my story of a young man who was a writer and found inspiration in our neighborhood. I know Tom would've liked that.

CYNICISM AND REALITY IN ADULTHOOD

Superman's Forest

"Her name is Melanie Monroe," I say to Steve, my partner, as he stares at the short, curvy blonde making her way toward us. We're on the back patio of our friendly neighborhood gay bar, IBT's on 4th Avenue. We hang out here every Saturday afternoon for happy hour and karaoke. "God. She was the biggest bitch in high school. Typical rich girl who went to Catholic school 'cuz Mom and Dad made her. Not a madonna or a whore, but somewhere right in between."

"Diego Martinez," Melanie says as she stops right next to my chair at the bar. "How the hell are ya?" She makes this odd snorting noise as she looks me up and down. After the once-over, she stares down at my feet and purses her lips at the sight of my leather sandals. She plops her oversized designer purse on the bar, right in the bartender's serving area. "I gotta go pee," she announces. "Watch my stuff." She doesn't wait for any response. She deserts her purse on the bar and heads toward the ladies room.

"What is she doing here?" Steve asks.

"I have no idea." I wait and watch as she enters the bathroom. "But I have a feeling she came here specifically to see me."

"Were you friends in high school?"

"Fuck no. Hated the bitch, and she hated me. Used to call me faggot all the time."

"But she came here to see you?"

"Let's just say we had a mutual boyfriend in high school."

"Oh yeah. You told me about him. Your first?"

"Yeah. Sixteen-year-old David Sunderson. He was something else. Star running back on the football team. Let's just say he had beautiful eyes." I stick out my two index fingers and hold them about ten inches apart. Steve laughs.

"Whatever happened to him?"

"Went to college on a football scholarship, and now I think he's a lawyer. Lives in town. I think he actually married Melanie. He married someone from high school, and I always thought it was her."

Melanie emerges from the bathroom. As she walks back toward us, she stares me directly in the eyes. Her gaze doesn't break mine. Her head is tilted forward, and her lips are still pursed together tightly. She appears as unfriendly as a cheetah stalking her prey, and I again wonder what the hell she wants from me.

"Melanie Monroe, this is my partner, Steve." I lean back in my chair so Steve can lean closer and shake her hand.

"Nice. You have a partner," Melanie replies, shakes Steve's hand, and adds, "I'm actually Melanie Sunderson."

"Nice," I reply. "So, you must have married David Sunderson."

"Yeah, married. Past tense. We just divorced last year."

"Wow. Sorry. You should take back your last name. Become Melanie Monroe again. I always loved your name."

"Yeah, I know I should. But we have two kids and I want to keep us all…well." She looks away. Her unfriendly stare is gone, and she stands next to me with both hands holding her large heavy purse down in front of her.

After a few seconds of silence, I ask, "Melanie, why are you here?"

"I don't know." She raises her right hand and pushes back the front of her hair. She holds her hair back, just over her forehead, and stares at me. "I heard you hang out here. I guess I just wanted to talk to you and see what this place was like." She looks around the bar unimpressed. "I really wanted to see what you were like now, and see what the people here were like." She sighs heavily, lets go of her hair, and it all falls back perfectly into place.

"Melanie?" I wait for her to look at me again. "Are you here to see what gay people are like? And what it's like in a gay bar?"

"That's part of it." She nods in agreement. Her unfriendly look has now been replaced by a look of guilt mixed with a large dose of curiosity.

"Part of what?"

Melanie's phone rings. It's in her large, ugly purse, and it's one of those ring tones that sounds like an old landline phone with the push button dials. "Wait," she says, as she opens her purse and rummages out her cell phone. "Shit. It's David. He has the kids, so I need to take this. I'm gonna go out to the parking lot, but I'll be back. Buy me a drink."

"Buy your own fucking drink."

"Buy me a drink, *faggot!*" she yells. As her phone continues to ring, she looks around at the five other people at the bar who are now staring back at her.

"She's kidding," I say.

Melanie stands silent with the loud phone in her hand. After a second, she answers it. "David. Just give me a second. I need to go somewhere where it's quiet. Hold on." She holds the phone to her side and makes her way to the door.

"What do you want to drink?" I yell back at her.

"Vodka martini, straight up, with a twist."

Ben, our favorite bartender, begins making her drink.

"Did you get that?" I ask Ben.

"Oh, yeah. I got it, *faggot*," Ben replies.

"So, what's her deal?" Steve asks as we both watch Ben make her martini and place it down in front of me.

"I don't know. We never really talked that much in high school. She was part of the uber popular crowd, while I was part of the middle crowd. You know? There were always more of us. We took up most of the school, but no one ever wanted to be us, and we all paid more attention to them. Besides, I was always drunk in high school. How do you think I was able to stay in the closet for so long?"

"So, she divorces this David Sunderson over a year ago, and now comes here to see you and talk to you about it. Strange chick," Steve adds, as we both stare at the back door of the bar.

Steve and I are sitting in "our corner," two tall stools at the end of a long metal bar. We're away from other people, but right next to the bartender's service area and usually surrounded by everyone else who works at the bar, a safe place where we can watch people, make comments, and sit in judgment. After a few drinks at happy hour, our singing gets a little bit better. But then, after a few more drinks at the end of happy hour, our singing quickly gets a little worse. Melanie took her phone and walked out the back door of the patio. I know she's in the parking lot talking with David, and I wonder if I have time to tell Steve much about David Sunderson.

"So, David's gay," I begin. "I bet he finally came out of the closet and divorced Melanie."

"Or got caught with another guy's dick in his mouth," Ben adds, wiping a glass as he leans in to hear more of my story.

"He and Melanie started dating in high school."

"When did you start seeing him?" Steve asks.

"He was never my boyfriend. He was always Melanie's boyfriend. He and I just used to meet every now and then and mess around."

"Every now and then?" Ben asks.

"Yeah," I say, trying to remember as much as I can about that year. "He was a senior when I was a junior. He'd always been friendly with me. He knew I was gay, and I knew he was curious. Really curious. So, we hooked up at the beginning of my junior year. You know...it was the mid-eighties. Nobody talked about being gay. I knew I could never come out of the closet, especially in high school, 'cuz I'd get the shit kicked out of me. Even in Catholic school, I knew someone would beat me up if I mentioned the word 'gay.' And then all of the priests and teachers would just look the other way."

"How did you guys finally hook up?" Steve asks.

"Is this exciting to you?"

"Kinda," he replies.

"High school sex is so cool," Ben adds.

"So, next to our little Catholic school was this vacant lot. It was kinda in the middle of the neighborhood, in between all of these big houses, and it was filled with oleanders and these big mesquite trees. We called it Superman's Forest. All the couples would go there to make out and be alone. I think there was even an old mattress in the back of the lot, but David and I never used it. It was really gross."

"You and David would hook up in Superman's Forest?" I can tell Steve's excitement is growing, and I just smile.

"Yeah." I place my left hand over my mouth and think. "I used to live by the school, and one day David followed me when I was walking home. Before I got to my house, I ducked into Superman's Forest and he followed me in. I didn't know if he would or not. But once he was there with me, he went for it. He went down on his knees and we started meeting in

Superman's Forest at least once a week. Let's just say that was a very good year."

"So it was a vacant lot surrounded by big houses?" Steve asks.

"Yeah," I reply. "You know the old neighborhood around the school? There was just this one piece of land between the houses. I mean, it had a lot of trees and bushes, and it really looked like a small forest. You had a lot of privacy once you were in it. I mean, no one could see you from the road or the surrounding houses. It was dense and kinda scary. I remember...you know...when David was servicing me, I'd stare up into the mesquite trees. The mesquites were pretty big, but they had these really long thorns, about three or four inches. These things looked like wooden dowels sticking out all over the branches and they were really sharp at the tips. David and I always called them the deadly mesquite trees. And then there were white oleanders all around. David always said how poisonous the flowers were, and then he'd pick a bunch and take them to Melanie. Nice, huh?"

"What a good gay boyfriend," Steve adds.

We all watch as Melanie walks back into the patio. She seems irritated and angry, but as far as I know, she always looks like that.

Steve gets down from his barstool and pulls it out for Melanie. "Here. Take my chair. I'm gonna go inside and see Richard. Let you two talk." With that, he goes to the inside bar.

"So, here's your martini," I say, pushing the drink in front of Melanie.

"Thanks."

Ben appears in front of us again and notices my empty beer bottle. "And you?" he asks. "Would you like another beer, Superman?"

"Fuck you."

"I'll take that as a yes."

"Yeah, and make it a double."

"How 'bout I just give you this one," Ben says, placing a new cold bottle down on the white napkin in front of me, "and back you up for the next one." He then places an upside down shot glass next to my beer.

"Thanks."

When Ben is standing at the opposite side of the bar, Melanie seems a bit more relaxed. She holds on to the stem of her martini glass but doesn't drink it. She slowly twirls the glass in front of her by its long stem and stares over at Ben, intently watching his every move. Again, she purses her lips together. "I know about you and David. In high school." Her eyes are still fixed on the opposite side of the bar. She stares at nothing with her lips pushed tightly together.

"What do you know about me and David?"

"That you used to blow him in Superman's Forest." She stops and watches her martini glass as she continues to slowly spin it in her hand. With a deep breath, Melanie picks up the glass and downs most of it.

I stop for a second and think about the approach I'm gonna take. I could lie to Melanie. Tell her everyone always made up rumors about me because I was different. Or tell her bits of the truth I've never told anyone before. How in the second grade everyone started calling me "fag" and how the name calling only stopped when I was in college. How my aunts and uncles even called me "sissy" or "weak" or "*joto*" when I was a little boy. Or how I had never kissed or even touched anyone until David followed me into Superman's Forest that one day.

In high school, I was afraid all the time. Fear filled my life, and suppression became my greatest talent. I would have never come on to David or talked to him about being gay because I was too afraid of getting caught. I was afraid of people finding out about me and letting everyone know that what they were saying about me was true. That Diego was a faggot. I was a faggot who was messing around with the most popular guy in high school, and I was loving every minute of it.

I pick up my beer and take a big swig. "Actually, Mel," I say. I know she hates it when people call her Mel, but I don't care. "My first time in Superman's Forest with David, *he* blew *me*. And he was really good at it."

Melanie looks up from her drink and stares me in the eyes. "Faggot," she says.

"Bitch."

"I knew it."

"What? That you're a bitch."

"No," she says. I can see tears in her eyes, but she starts to laugh. "Well, yes, I'm a bitch. I'm a bitch, Diego. Is that what you want to hear? I don't know what the fuck I'm doing here, and I feel like a total bitch because I had to see you and find out the truth. Hear it from you directly."

"Well, the truth is what? Twenty-seven years ago, I messed around with your ex-husband in high school."

"No," she says. She wipes the tears from her eyes but still continues to smile. "I guess that you knew the truth about David for twenty-seven years, and I just found out about it two years ago."

"Melanie, I'm sorry. I don't know what to say."

"No," she begins. "I wanted to hear it from you, and now I have. But let me ask you this." She tilts her head back and blinks away more tears. She exhales and breathes in again slowly. "I know you probably don't want to talk about this, but did you ever get married after high school?"

"You mean to a woman?"

"Yes, to a woman."

"No. I never wanted to be with a woman, ever."

"Then if David knew he was gay when he was fucking around with you in high school, why did he marry me?" Melanie laughs. It's an uncomfortable laugh—uncomfortable for her and really uncomfortable for me. It sounds forced out of her, like the question that's apparently been driving her crazy for quite some time. She exhales slowly and breathes in again. "Please, Diego. All I'm looking for is some kind of answer."

"I don't know." I finish my beer and push the upside-down shot glass forward. I know I need another one. "Melanie, it was the eighties. He was in the closet. Everyone I knew was in the closet, especially in Catholic school. Come on."

"But in high school, you were different. Everyone knew you were gay, but no one ever talked about it. And it was like you didn't care."

"I fucking hated high school, because I knew it was not for me. I was terrible at all that social shit in high school. I was lucky, though. I knew my life would change in college, and I just worked my way through high school knowing I would go away to college and leave all that shit behind me. And I drank a lot too, so that helped." Ben places my next beer down in front of me. With a quick nod from me, he again places the upside-down shot glass back on the bar next to my beer.

"Did your life change in college?"

"Yeah!" I stop myself because I know I'm starting to shout. "I didn't need to fit in in college, I just needed to do well. And I did. I mean I got my bachelor's and then went back for my master's and I just finished my PhD last year. I liked college a lot, I guess. I did spend about fifteen years getting my degrees."

"So you're…"

"Yeah. On campus, I'm Dr. Martinez."

"And what do you do for a living?"

"I teach over in the graduate college at U of A."

"You teach what?"

"I teach technical and professional writing. I'm mainly a writer. I write a bunch of fiction, stories, and books, but my real job is teaching writing to undergraduate research students. I show them how to document their work in written reports and journal articles for presentation and publication."

"Nice," Melanie says, ordering another martini.

"What about you, Melanie?" I sit up straight in my chair and lean closer to her. "What do you do when David's not around?"

"I sell real estate." She stops and watches Ben place a new martini in front of her. "And I'm a full-time mom. David's good with the kids, but taking care of them is all my responsibility."

I look away from Melanie, and there's another uncomfortable silence. I know she wants me to answer her question, but I'm just not quite sure what I want to say. I think about David and what he was like in high school. I try to imagine what David is like now, as a forty-five-year-old man just coming out of the closet and starting his life as an out and proud gay man. I try, but I can't remember anything about David's family or what his life was like away from school. We never talked about stuff like that. All we did was mess around.

While David was considerate and affectionate while we were together in Superman's Forest, I never really saw him or spoke to him outside of the forest. David was a different person when we were behind the trees, and we always avoided seeing each other at school. David would do his thing, and I would do mine. And then we'd hook up in Superman's Forest, and that was our release. The forest was our safe place, where we could be gay boys who enjoyed each other's company. We could be alone together, away from the world and what we were expected to be. We could be young homosexuals who really didn't talk, but definitely knew how to please each other and have a good time together.

"Melanie," I begin. "You're the one who knows David best. My God, you just spent the last twenty-seven years together. You know he must have married you because he loved you. Don't you?"

"I don't know. David loves himself and his perfect little life."

"You're a part of his perfect little life. You're the wife who helped him get to where he is today. Look, Melanie." I lean forward and place both of my elbows on the bar. I try to look her in the face, but she's still staring forward, watching Ben's every move. "As American men, we're raised with this expectation of who and what we are to be in life. Everyone expects a young man to marry the perfect young woman, get a job, buy a house, pop out a few kids, and mow his fucking lawn the rest of his life. I think it was just a lot easier for David to give in to that life and those expectations. I mean, that's what he's achieved with you, right? You're the perfect wife, he's got the perfect job, and I'm thinking he's got perfect kids.

"But what kind of life does he have now? He still has you as his perfect first wife with his perfect little family. And he still has you to help him maintain that part of his life. But now he's out of the closet, and he's still able to enjoy a great deal of the life you helped him establish."

Melanie stares forward and begins to slowly spin her martini again.

"A lot of married couples divorce and go on to have separate lives, but they still share their lives with their first spouses. Especially if there are children involved. What makes you and David and your relationship any different now that he's admitted to being gay? Did he cheat on you? Or are you upset that he lied to you and pretended to be something he's not?"

"He never cheated on me," Melanie replies, oddly calm. She looks away from Ben. She turns her head toward me but stares away from my face. "At least he said he never cheated on me. He said the only man he's ever been with is you."

"Wow," I reply. I didn't mean to say anything. The word just slipped out of my mouth and I'm kinda regretting it now. "Anyway, go on."

"He told me, Diego." She lifts her head, now staring me directly in the eyes. She purses her lips together again, and I can see that hungry and determined look on her face. "He said he knew he was going to be okay. I mean be okay coming out of the closet now, because he knows there are gay men like you in the world. Somehow, he knows you're in a relationship. He knows about you and Steve, and that you've been together a long time. He said he didn't want to try and start a relationship with you, but he wants to find someone just like you. And have a relationship like you and Steve."

"Wow." There it is again. I clench my teeth together, not knowing what else to say.

"That's also why I wanted to find you. I wanted to know what you're like now, and I wanted to meet Steve. I guess I wanted to have a better understanding of what's happening to David, and what he's looking for now."

"Wow." I'm dumbfounded and literally can't think of anything else to say. I just look down and drink my beer.

After a few more seconds of silence, Melanie adds, "Yeah, so that's all I really wanted to say. I can see you're all freaked out, so I'm gonna go back to my perfectly fucked-up little life and leave you alone."

"Wow." This time I say it in a long, drawn-out tone.

"Great, Diego. Thanks, you've been really helpful." She

leans forward on the bar and pulls her heavy purse closer to her. "Good luck with the teaching and the writing. Maybe you can even write a little story about you, me, and David. That is, if you get hard up for something to write about."

I continue to stare forward.

"Just do me a favor." She stops and waits for some kind of a reply from me. I turn and stare at her. "Just don't make me out to be a big bitch, okay? You know, like how you used to always call me a bitch in high school."

"Oh, honey," I reply. I purse my lips together tightly, trying to hold back my smile. I step down from my barstool and swig the rest of my beer. "I'm a good writer, but I ain't that good." I pick up my upside-down shot glass, smile, and head for the inside bar. I need to find Steve and tell him the rest of the story.

McCarran Airport

I am people watching again, sitting at the gate waiting for our plane to arrive. An older couple is making their way to the door of the men's bathroom.

"Look at that couple."

"What couple?" Dan looks up from his Kindle and scans the terminal.

"In front of the men's room." I push my chin forward in their direction. "Over there."

"What about them?"

"Something's wrong." The old man leads his wife to one side of the open entrance to the bathroom. "He's holding her arm so tightly, and he's just dragging her around."

"Yeah." Dan watches with me. "Something is wrong."

"But look at her. I don't think she knows where she is." The older woman stares forward, away from her husband. "What do you think?"

"Alzheimer's?"

"Yeah. I was thinking it might be something like that. But just look at the husband."

"He looks exhausted."

"And desperate."

"So, what are you thinking?"

"I'm thinking he needs to go pee, but he doesn't want to leave her outside alone."

"Yeah, he does look desperate."

"Sorry." I look over at Dan, knowing he hates it when I get involved. "I'm gonna go over and see if I can help." I'm out of my chair.

"Andrew, wait."

"Watch our stuff." I look back at him. "I'll just be right over there. We need to let the guy go pee."

"Oh...kay." Dan smirks.

The closer I get to the older man, the more I can see he is on the verge of tears. I don't know what I'm doing. All I know is I want to help.

"Hi," I say to the man as I stop right next to him. I smile at his wife and wonder how I can get her to trust me enough to let her husband leave her for three minutes to use the restroom. "I'm Andrew." The older woman looks up but stares past me. I smile at her. "Has anyone ever told you that you look like Barbara Stanwyck?"

The woman blinks her eyes. Looking at me again, it's as if her eyes have come back into focus and she really sees me. "I love Barbara Stanwyck." Her whole face brightens.

"With your white hair, you look just like her." I smile as brightly as possible. "When I was a kid, I used to love her TV show, *The Big Valley*. I watched it every afternoon. And my mom is a huge Barbara Stanwyck fan, so we used to watch her old movies all the time."

The woman does look like Barbara Stanwyck, so I am not making anything up. Not as Stanwyck looked in *The Big Valley*, but more how she looked later on in her career like in *The Thorn Birds* or when she'd show up on *Dynasty*.

"Barbara Stanwyck," she says again.

"You know, my favorite movie of hers is one called *Remember the Night*."

The woman gasps. "With Fred MacMurray?"

"Yeah, Fred MacMurray. I love that movie." I glance over at her husband, who stares back at me with a complete look of disbelief. "Do you need to use the restroom?" I place my hand lightly at the small of his back. "I can stay here and talk with your wife if you need to go."

"Yes," he replies. He still looks as if he's on the verge of tears, but he turns away and slowly walks into the bathroom.

I want to focus on the past and engage the woman's long-term memory, so I add, "Every Christmas we always watch *Christmas in Connecticut*. That's also one of our favorites."

"People..." She stops. She furrows her brow, takes her time, and begins again. "People always told me I looked like Stanwyck." She stares past me but smiles.

After a few more minutes of me racking my brain for any Barbara Stanwyck film I can think of, her husband appears behind her.

"We've been having a great conversation."

"You okay?" The husband maneuvers his face in front of his wife's eyes. When she looks at him and smiles, he sighs heavily. Still looking at her, he adds, "Thank you."

"It's nothing."

"No." He takes her by the elbow again. This time his grip is much lighter. "All of her life people have always told her she looks like Barbara Stanwyck. At her old job they even called her Victoria Barkley. Well, I mean, back in the sixties. You know, like on *The Big Valley*."

"That's the first thing that struck me when I walked over here." I let out a small laugh. The wife begins to stare forward at nothing again. I look at his hand on her elbow and notice his grip has tightened.

"Are you going to be okay getting to your plane? If we can help…"

The husband lowers his eyebrows and looks around. "We?"

"Yeah." I look back over toward Dan. "My partner and I are traveling home to Tucson. We've been here in Vegas for three days, and that's long enough for us."

"Partner?"

"Yeah. That's Dan over there." I wave my hand at him. "Wave back at me, Dan."

Dan sits up and waves.

"You two are in business together?"

"No."

The man shakes his head confused and looks as if I'm speaking a foreign language.

"Dan and I are gay." Now the man looks as if he has taken a big bite out of a large juicy lemon that has been dipped in Tabasco sauce and rolled around in shattered glass. I can't help myself, and I let out a short, nervous laugh. "Yeah. I call Dan my partner because we share a life together. I mean, I don't call him my husband because we're not married. We've just never gotten around to making it all official."

"Yeah." The man stops. "I guess that is legal for guys like you these days."

"Yeah, that whole Supreme Court thing allowing us the same civil rights as others."

"Civil rights…" The man laughs.

"Yeah." I'm dumbfounded. These days, people don't call you faggot to your face or tell you you're going to hell for your "chosen" lifestyle. They just make that face, turn as if they have never spoken to you, and walk away. Again, I don't know what I'm doing, but I can't stay quiet. I wait for the man to look at me. He doesn't. So, I look back at his wife. "It was great meeting you, Barbara Stanwyck. And I hope you have a safe trip home." She focuses on me again.

"Barbara Stanwyck." She smiles and looks as if she's remembering an old friend. "And Fred MacMurray." She points her finger at me.

"Me?" I laugh.

"Yes."

"No."

The husband stares at his wife as if he's hearing her speak for the first time in weeks. He's let go of her elbow and stands cautiously at her side, eagerly awaiting her next move.

"I don't know about that. I'm no Fred MacMurray." I shake my head and think of the movie *Double Indemnity* where Barbara Stanwyck had Fred MacMurray kill her husband. I stare at the old man from head to toe. His white cotton shirt and dark blue pants make him so conservative and nondescript. But the way he stares at his wife, focuses on her face, and leans ever so slightly in her direction shows me he's spent a lifetime loving this woman. A woman who does look amazingly like Barbara Stanwyck. And a wife who probably never questioned her husband's thinking or his motives. I again let out a short, nervous laugh. At this point I can't control myself. "Let's just say I am more like a Montgomery Clift kind of guy."

"I love Montgomery Clift." She still focuses on me.

"And Montgomery Clift loves you, too."

"I haven't seen her like this in months." The husband looks at his wife as if time has somehow played a trick on him and allowed her to become ten years younger. He smiles brightly as she stares up at me. The husband exhales deeply as he watches her reach her hand up and brush it slightly against the side of my face.

After a few seconds of silence, the wife turns away and stares at nothing again.

"Look, I don't really care what you think about me or my life as a gay man. I just want to make sure she gets on your plane, so if you need help, I'm here to help you in any way possible."

"She's been like this for over a year." He holds her at the elbow once again. "She has dementia, and she's had a stroke. Some days are good and some days are...but this? This has been a good day." Tears well up in his eyes, and he blinks them away. "If you can just help us locate our gate and see if the desk people will help us get on the plane. That'd help me out a lot."

"Sure."

After reading their boarding passes, guiding them to their gate, and making sure they would receive assistance when boarding their plane, I return to Dan.

"Did you help?" he asks.

"As much as I could."

"Did he not like homosexuals?"

"You heard?"

"Oh, yeah. I could hear him from here."

"But I won him over."

"You always do."

"Me and my magic, that's all it takes."

"You and what? Your magic dust?"

"Yes." I let out a longer, much less nervous laugh. "The kind of magic dust that can only come from a fairy like me."

TUCKER

My writing is not flowing, so I sit back in my bench and stare at the people around me. Couples sit in the park, eating their lunches and discussing their days. A few kids play in the grass, and young professionals are taking a midday break. I want to go back to my story and write at least the first five hundred words, but it is not happening. I close my laptop and stare down at my hands. They look dried, cracked, and old. I grip my laptop at either end, moving the tops of my hands underneath it to hide my bulging veins and ashy red knuckles. The ugly, brown hands of a fifty-year-old.

Still looking down, I hear a man's voice yell out, "Tucker! What the hell do ya think you're doing?"

Tucker is a young boy, no older than five. He is a small, angelic child, thin and pale white, with sandy blond hair and bright blue eyes. I'm sure the moment his father parked their truck and his mom opened the passenger door, Tucker made a break for it. He ran as fast as he could to get away from his parents. And as he continues to run, he looks as if he's running toward nothing. The swing set is in the opposite direction. The large grassy field is to his right. But the small boy just runs directly toward me and stops at the edge of the parking lot. He looks around himself, taking it all in. I just laugh at the boy. He smiles at himself and what he's just gotten away with.

"Tucker!" his father yells again, and the young boy's smile disappears. His shoulders tense up, and he stares away from his father. "What do you think you're doing, gawking at all the people like that? You look like an idiot. Come back here, idiot-boy, and help your mother with lunch."

Tucker turns and looks at me with a blank stare. He spins around, and with a burst of energy, runs to the door of the camper on the back of his father's truck. Tucker's father is a heavyset man, dressed in black work boots, faded Levi's, and a gray wifebeater that must have been white at one time. He looks older than he probably is, with a full head of gray hair and a goatee that's black at the chin and gray around the mustache.

"Don't run off like that! What were you thinking?" The father looks over at me. He places his hand on top of Tucker's head, gives me half a smile, and pushes his son back toward the truck.

As I sit on my bench, at one end of the park, I let go of my laptop and look away. I know I'm staring directly at this little family, so I slide closer to one side of the bench. I look around desperately at the rest of the park, trying to fix my eyes on the opposite side of the street, but I keep turning back and looking for Tucker.

Tucker's father drives a beat-up Chevy truck that sits alone in the parking lot. The truck is white and dented and looks as if it's been through a lot in its short lifetime. In the bed of the truck is a homemade camper shell that looks like a large wooden doghouse. Its pitched roof leans oddly to one side, thick, dark shingles cover the top, and a dark brown door serves as its opening. The door is held shut by a makeshift lock that looks like an oddly shaped wire hanger. But above the door, written in bright red letters, shining in the midday sun, is the word *Home* on a hand-painted sign.

As I try to stare past the family into the park, the father's loud, dramatic voice keeps calling my attention back. The man is projecting his voice, and everything he says is clear and deliberate. He knows he has an audience, with me close by on the bench, and I wonder why he cares so much about my attention or what I think of him and his family.

"Tucker, go help your mother with the food." The man's hand is at the small of Tucker's back. But as Tucker moves toward his mother, the man grips on to the back of his shirt and holds him still. "You're such a good boy." He pulls Tucker closer to his side, gives the boy a half-baked hug, and pats him on the head. "Such a good boy. Now, go and help your mommy."

Tucker's mother has already unhinged the wire hanger and opened the back door of the camper. Without a word, she helps the young boy into the camper and hops in herself. The father turns, glances at me, and then looks around the rest of the park. I turn away and decide to open up my laptop again. I feel a bit of inspiration coming on.

Just as I open my computer, I hear someone call my name behind me.

"Hey, Ernesto."

I turn around and see my younger cousin, David, walking toward me. David is my second cousin, one of about seventy-two first and second cousins I have in Arizona and Mexico, mainly Mexico City. David is eighteen, and he is preparing to go to college at the end of the summer. David looks a lot like my grandfather, the first American Quintanilla, who walked to the United States from Mexico during the Mexican Revolution. But David is a new and improved version. With his light hazel eyes, dark brown hair, and skin that turns red rather than brown in the Arizona sun, he is a beautiful young Mexican-American.

I was never close to David when he was a child, as I was in and out of school, earning my PhD and establishing my career at the university. And while I am not close to any of my cousins, David and I have been talking a lot recently. While David is what I consider to be the perfect son, with his straight As in high school and a full academic scholarship to college, he is considered less than ideal in a family like mine. David, like me, is a homosexual.

He came out to his mother when he was sixteen years old. He didn't mean to, but she caught him in their garage with his pants around his ankles and his dick in the mouth of his eighteen-year-old boyfriend. Before sharing this information with his father or anyone else in our extended family, she brought him to me—dropped him off at my office and said David needed to get to know me. Me, the only openly gay member of our entire clan; the only one who's not fathered or given birth to three or more children; the only one who's completed a college degree and went on to earn a PhD in English; and possibly the only one who can help David understand who and what he is.

"Hola, Ernesto," David says as he walks around the bench and sits down next to me.

We exchange greetings, but something is bothering him. "So, *joto*, what brings you here on this fine day?"

David laughs. "I wanted to talk about more college stuff."

"More college stuff?" I lean in closer to him. "Or did you want to talk about more family stuff?"

David smiles. He looks over at Tucker's father's truck. He lowers his eyebrows, looks up and down at the wooden camper shell, and shakes his head. "Yeah," he sighs, still gazing forward. "I wanted to talk about more family stuff."

"I thought so." I wait for him to look back at me, but he doesn't. He keeps his eyes on the truck. "Tell me how things are going with you and your father."

"Oh…" David stares forward at the truck and exhales. "He tolerates me."

"That's good, right? At least he hasn't disowned you or sent you to a camp where they try and fix young gay men."

"I guess."

"You know, they sent me to a camp like that when I was young. But I got kicked out. I ended up in bed with my camp counselor. Let's just say I'm the one who gave him the title of Head Counselor."

"You're so full of shit."

"Yeah, I am. But I made you laugh." David continues to stare forward. "I got to say, at your age I was afraid of everything and everyone." My throat tightens and my eyes water up.

David has made more progress coming out than I did at his age. When I was younger, I remember fearing for my safety in the hallways of my high school as bullies relentlessly called me faggot; crying hysterically after my uncle slapped me across the face for mentioning John Travolta was cute; or driving away to college with the word *joto* spray-painted on the tailgate of my truck by a few members of my extended family. "And here you are," I say, "going away to college as an out and proud gay man." I think about turning away and not letting David see my emotions, but I don't. I want him to see how speaking with him about his life and future continues to affect me.

He clears his throat, straightens his back, and sits up in the bench. "How did you tell your nana and tata you were gay?" David leans toward me and places his elbows on his knees.

I came out when I was thirty-one. David wasn't even born then. That happened the next year, when most of my extended family was not speaking to me, and I had decided to go away to college again and earn my master's degree. While my immediate family is close, and we try our best to love and support one another, my extended family is competitive, and we try our best to outdo one another or call attention to the weaknesses of others. Fucked up? Yes. Not heeding our Christian/Catholic faith? Yes. But it's what I have come to know as family.

I had made the decision to return for my master's to put some distance between me and my extended family. I also wanted to live alone and discover who I really was. But a year before all of that, I took my parents out to dinner, had a few too many vodka tonics, and told them I was gay. They took the news well. They didn't disown me, didn't mention anything to the extended family, and didn't send me away to Camp Gay Cure. They told me I was their son, and they loved me. And when it was over, I wondered why I was so afraid to tell my mother and father. And what was it about coming out as a gay man that made me question my parents' acceptance and love of me.

Since then, I have always thought it was just plain fear, based on what everyone else thought about me and my life, rather than trusting in my parents' love and seeing them for who and what they really are—two individuals who love me dearly; who would never push me out of their lives because they did not understand who I was; and who would always defend me when anyone questioned what I wanted.

Coming out to my parents was the most important decision I've ever made, and it saddens me to think David did not have the same experience with his parents. While his mother, my cousin Gina, responded to him in the same way as my parents, his father, who is a Quintanilla, pushed him away and said very little. Tolerance is the word David uses when speaking of his father and their relationship. David is spending less and less time with his father and will probably not see him again before he leaves for college. Being that David and I are from two different generations, it also saddens me his progress can be dampened by a father who cannot see him as the gift he truly is.

Still contemplating my own story, I look over into the parking lot and see Tucker standing outside the camper shell. His mother has loaded him down with plates, cups, bottles of ketchup and mustard, and a large fork and spatula for the barbecue. The poor kid stands motionless, trying to keep everything balanced in his arms.

"Tucker!" his father yells from behind him, and that's it. Everything in his arms comes crashing down to the ground. "Can't you do anything right, boy?" His father pushes him to one side, and Tucker falls toward the back bumper of the truck. He steadies himself with his right arm against the chrome bumper, and tears well up in his eyes.

"Don't cry, boy!" his father yells, then turns toward us. David and I look at each other and then back at Tucker and his father.

"It's okay. It's okay." His father grabs Tucker by the arm and holds him still. "I love you. I love you, little boy. And everything is going to be okay. Just pick up all this shit and meet me over there by the barbecue grill." His father lets go of his arm and points at one of the old, rusted public barbecue grills. Looking back at us, the father smiles, pulls a Zippo lighter out of his pocket, and walks into the park.

"So, you're worried about coming out to your nana?" I ask in response to his question.

"Yeah," David replies, still fixing his eyes on Tucker and watching the boy as he goes over to his father. Leaning back in the bench again, David adds, "My father gets his conservative side, all of his holier-than-thou shit from my nana. So, I'm worried about telling her I'm gay and how she'll react."

I think of my Tía Rosa, David's nana, and what a pistol she's been all her life.

Tía Rosa raised two sons on her own, working as a maid and later as a waitress. She never married the father of her boys, but she set herself up to be the most conservative, staunch Catholic in the family. Uneducated and truly judgmental is how we all describe her. Now she lives on Social Security, readily utilizes every aspect of her Medicare, and proudly calls herself a strict Republican.

"Honestly," I say, "I just let everyone else figure it out on their own." I look away from David and stare over at Tucker's camper shell of a house. It's deserted now, with the family eating lunch in the park, and I fixate on the sign that reads *Home*.

"I remember feeling like my coming out of the closet was never going to stop. We're a huge family, and we all have a large number of friends. But I remember after telling my youngest sister, I decided I was going to stop coming out. Coming out can be a really emotional thing. And to keep doing it again and again and again. My God, it can get so... At one point, I'd decided I'd had enough. I'd told all the people I loved, so I just stopped. I had done what I needed to do, and I wasn't going to share that experience with anyone else.

"Steve and I have been together now for, let's see...He hates it when I can't get the number right, but I think we've been together for sixteen years. So, instead of coming out of the closet again and again, I'd just introduce them to Steve. That's really how I handled coming out to the rest of the family. Quite frankly, I don't give a shit what they think of me. And coming out of the closet gets exhausting. Like everything else in life, you need to prioritize. Do you need to come out to your nana? Do know how she will react? Or do you know you can't do anything about that reaction and want to spare yourself that drama?"

"There's always that point in our conversations when I feel like I'm not only talking with my cousin and good friend, Ernesto, but I'm also talking with Dr. Quintanilla," David replies.

"I know. I can be a bit cut-and-dried when I want to be. They taught me that in graduate school. Plus, my students tend to appreciate my frankness."

"But don't you think I should give my nana the opportunity to get to know me?"

"What? She doesn't already know you?"

"Yeah, but I feel like I should give her the benefit of the doubt and hope she'll say she loves me and wants me to be happy."

"Just like your father and his reaction?"

"Shit."

"Exactly." I hear voices again, and I figure it must be Tucker and his family, but I keep my attention fixed on David. "For me, coming out of the closet really meant I was living my life on my own terms, and I never again wanted to pretend to be something I'm not. The hard part was understanding those feelings of disappointment. And that I could control who I let disappoint me."

"So, you think my nana will disappoint me?"

"No. That's not what I'm saying. What I want is for you to take control and set your priorities. One priority being that you stop being so disappointed by others."

"So what? Build a wall around myself?"

"Maybe." I laugh at how much I appreciate David's intelligence. "By coming out of the closet, you are asking people to accept you for who you are. So, why don't you accept others for who they are, and spend a little more time sparing yourself the ravages of this large, judgmental, and often disappointing family?"

"Ay, nana," David replies.

"Ay, Tía Rosa," I add.

David and I sit together in silence for quite some time. Tucker's family finishes their lunch and packs everything back into the truck. Tucker's father shuts the back door of the camper shell and fixes the wire hanger to hold it shut. Without looking back at us, he walks over to the driver's side of the truck and gets in. The truck rolls backward and turns with the passenger's window toward us. Tucker sits on his mother's lap, staring at us with his bright blue eyes. He's starting to cry. David looks over at me, but I still stare into the watery eyes of the small angelic boy. The truck stands still in front of us, and the young boy leans away from his mother and closer to the window. He raises his right hand in front of him and looks as if he's waving goodbye, but the truck lurches forward and the boy braces himself against the passenger window with his flattened hand. He steadies himself in his mother's lap and continues to cry.

Without a word, David raises his hand to the boy and waves goodbye. The truck lurches forward one more time and, with a burst of acceleration, drives out of the parking lot.

After a few seconds, David says, "I gotta go."

"Will I see you again before you leave for school?"

"Yeah. Let's do dinner or something." He gives me half a smile.

"Great," I reply. "And David," I catch him before he can walk away, "are you going to tell your nana that you're gay?"

"No." He turns his head and stares down at me. "I think I'll go to college first."

"Great," I reply again. David turns and takes a few steps

away. "And David," I add, "you saw yourself in that little boy, didn't you?"

"Yeah, I did."

"You know you're not a little boy anymore, right?"

"I know," he replies and before walking away adds, "but people still push me around, and it hurts."

Paul and Cézanne

Paul stood perfectly still in front of the painting. Dozens of people would come and go around him, but he remained in his one favorite spot, almost as if he had become yet another motionless piece of art in the museum. Fifteen or twenty minutes would go by, and he would hold steady in his place. He only moved his eyes over the oil on canvas, staring at the details of the lone man sitting inside the frame. It was the ninth time this month Paul had come to the Musée d'Orsay, and it was the twelfth week of his and his family's stay in Paris.

Paul had first come to the museum as an American tourist to see all of the beautiful artwork the Musée had to offer. He'd walk through the five floors with his museum map in hand and listen through white earbuds to a black handheld radio device. The recording provided details about some of the artists and great works throughout the museum, but Paul returned just to visit the artwork on the fifth floor in the Galerie des Impressionnistes. He wanted to revisit the work, spend more time with his favorite pieces, and abandon the small radio device. He wanted to walk the floor and see what details he could remember on his own. And, finally, Paul returned a few more times to revisit the one painting that held him so captivated. His one favorite painting by Cézanne.

The painting was called *Le Joueur de Cartes*. It pictured a man sitting at one end of a plain, square table. He was playing cards. The man wore a dark brown coat, something between a suit jacket and an overcoat. The garment added girth to the man's frame, and Paul wondered if underneath the heavy coat the man was well fed or terribly thin. The man also wore a hat the exact same brown color as the jacket. The entire brim of the hat was folded upward, encircling the top of the man's head. But the man's face fascinated Paul the most. And it was his face that kept drawing Paul back to the painting, examining it from every angle.

The skin on the man's face was red and brown. The red looked like some recent tanning from working outdoors, and the brown resembled a mixture of the man's ethnic background along with years and years of exposure to harsh sunlight. The man's features, his jet black hair, black bushy eyebrows, and thick heavy mustache, are what reminded Paul the most of his family. Those are what made the man look like a Quintanilla. But the man's docile expression, his focus on his cards, and his dark-colored attire reminded Paul of his tata. And they comforted Paul as he stood in the presence of the painting, despite the exhaustion and loneliness he felt outside of the museum in his temporary home with Sean and their two children here in Paris.

Sean had asked Paul to come to Paris with him eight months ago, so Paul had packed up the essentials, locked up their house, and moved them all to Paris. All of them. Their cute little family: Paul, Sean, and their two three-year-old sons. Sean was an actor and been cast in his first movie role. He was to play the wisecracking gay bartender in a major studio film being shot in the Montparnasse area. It was a supporting role, but this was supposed to be Sean's big break. And he kept telling Paul that. "This is it. This is my big break. We have to go!" So Paul agreed to the move with one major stipulation; they would hire an *au pair* in Paris to help him with the kids.

After nine years in their committed relationship, Paul and Sean had adopted twin boys. And after twelve years of acting on the stage in Houston, Sean had been given this big break. And Paul, who was sick of his life in retail sales and his constant search for a better career, had agreed to follow him to Paris. But soon found himself alone, visiting the attractions, wandering the streets, and waiting for Sean to stop working all the time.

Paul saw all the major attractions his first week in Paris: the Eiffel Tower, the Louvre, Notre Dame, and the Arc de Triomphe. He walked endlessly up and down the Champs-Élysées not quite sure what he was looking for. Along the Champs-Élysées, Paul decided to stop shopping and just take in all the details of Paris. This became his entertainment for days.

The Champs-Élysées was by far the widest street Paul had found in Paris, with roomy sidewalks made of gray concrete blocks that moved slightly when you walked over them. Tall, green trees lined the side of the street closest to the Arc de Triomphe, perfectly groomed to look like thin, square columns moving you into the exclusive shopping area.

The men along the Champs-Élysées held Paul's attention for days. There were the older, or even middle-aged men who looked like businessmen you could readily spot in London, New York, or even Washington DC. These men walked along the street always looking as if they had somewhere to go. The younger men worked along the Champs-Élysées, mainly in the fashion industry or in the exclusive and expensive shops in the area.

These men wore tight-fitting clothes, shiny silver or light blue suits that accentuated their painfully thin bodies and looked as if they were one size too small. They kept their jackets open in the front. They had buttons on one side and corresponding button holes on the other, but they were never really meant to hold the jacket closed. These fashionable young men also wore custom slip-on leather shoes with no laces or buckles. They were almost always light brown and looked longer than they needed to be, with sharp, pointed tips that appeared to reach beyond the toes of the foot inside.

Every now and then, Paul would notice men who were not from Paris or probably not even from France. The American men wore big, baggy shorts, baseball caps, and white tennis shoes. These men bored Paul, and he'd often roll his eyes and groan, "Ay...Americans." Then there were the dark, rugged men who were extremely physically fit. These men would wear tight black cotton T-shirts, thick black leather belts, heavy black work boots, and faded cargo pants that were a light golden brown. They wore their clothes as if they were some kind of uniform, and Paul thought they might be from some Eastern European country. They usually smoked, had dark features, facial hair that was just beyond stubble, and a tattoo on the inside of one forearm.

These brooding men walked the streets of Paris with a silent and stern determination. They excited Paul, and quite a few times he found himself following one up and down the Champs-Élysées. But he knew with a husband and two children, he'd always have to behave himself. Even if Sean was busy seven days a week, twelve to fifteen hours a day, Paul knew he had to be faithful. That was the agreement they made right after their commitment ceremony, on their honeymoon: always keep your dick in your pants and your tongue in your mouth. Paul hoped it was a mutual agreement.

Eventually Paul made his way beyond the Champs-Élysées and wandered throughout the Montparnasse area where he and

Sean had rented a small apartment. On his midday walks, Paul marveled at the number of large motorcycles that dominated the streets of Paris. They often had two fat wheels in front, making them look like a backward tricycle for adults, and they were covered in black plastic, with storage compartments around the back wheel and heavy black plastic covering the wheels in front.

There were also destitute men, and Paul couldn't tell if the down-and-out men he saw were actually homeless, or just poor, hungry men standing on the streets asking for assistance. They were often dressed in long cardigan sweaters that hung to their knees with amazingly clean light cotton pants. They would lean up against a wall on a street corner that was not too busy and hold up a thin fishing pole with a white Dixie cup tied to the end of the line. They did not say a word, but simply maneuvered the Dixie cup in front of you as you walked by.

Paul also saw young women on the streets of Paris. They had raggedy black hair and were dressed in black jeans and dirty white T-shirts. They pushed petitions at you, asking you to sign your name and somehow support them. They were Deaf, or pretended to be Deaf, but emphatically urged you to sign their sheet of paper. These women terrified Paul, so he never stopped to see what their petitions said or found out what they really wanted from the strangers who passed them by.

In his third week, Paul finally ventured into the many other museums in Paris. At first, he sought out the Musée Picasso, which was incredibly hard to find amongst the narrow, winding streets of the Marais district. But when he did find it, its plain green doorway displayed a simple little sign that said it was closed for remodeling for the next two years.

Paul eventually located the Musée de l'Orangerie in the corner of the Tuileries Gardens. Both the gardens and the museum were beautiful and tranquil, especially the small musée that housed Monet's massive murals of the water lilies.

And, finally, Paul sought out the Musée d'Orsay, on the left bank of the Seine, where he discovered his beloved painting by Cézanne. At first Paul had bought a museum pass that allowed him access to all the museums for one week, and he found himself visiting the Musée d'Orsay four times before it expired. After that, he went to the museum three times in one week, standing in the presence of the Cézanne holding a day pass. He stood in that one spot for at least an hour, remembering his tata, thinking of his family, feeling like he was home, and enjoying a sense of being there.

Paul made friends with one of the female guards on the fifth floor of the Musée d'Orsay in the Galerie des Impressionnistes. The museum guards usually sat in silence, observed the patrons, and kept them from making too much noise or taking pictures of the artwork, but Odette wanted to practice her English on the friendly, young gay American. Paul just wanted to take over her chair and get off his feet since it was located directly in front of Paul's beloved Cézanne.

The sturdy, dark red chair was made of a heavy, clear plastic you could see through, with white feet at the bottom that covered the large bolts holding the chair securely to the floor. Sitting in the chair, Paul always felt relieved staring at the painting and visiting with his tata. His tata always listened to him and accepted him for who he was. His tata who would have helped him think through what he and Sean were going through here in Paris.

As Paul sat down in the clear plastic red chair one last time, he thought of his third week in Paris when he found Sean in the corner of their apartment, staring at the wall. Paul had just put the kids to bed, sent the *au pair* out for her weekend away, and found Sean this way. Sean's eyes were tired and bloodshot, and he had a large pink and red spot in the middle of his forehead. Often, when Sean would get upset about anything, particularly his career, he would flatten his hand as much as possible, rock back and forth in a crouched position on the floor, and beat his head with the bottom of his palm again and again until he had a doughnut-sized red spot just above two equally red and wary eyes.

"You don't understand," was Sean's constant message. "You will never fucking understand." He said it so often, Paul now hated the sound of it in his head.

The first time he found Sean like that, Paul had asked, "Sean? You okay? What is it this time?"

"I can't...I just can't."

"You can't what?"

"I can never make them happy." His breathing was erratic, and he stared at nothing. "I just can't ever make them happy."

"Happy with what?" Paul knew it was a stupid question and regretted it once it left his mouth. Sean shot back an evil stare that reinforced his constant message: Paul didn't understand his work or the amount of pressure he dealt with as an actor making his first big-budget movie with people who actually came from Hollywood.

"They fucking hate me!"

"Well..." Paul stopped, exhaled, and thought about his words carefully. "Sean, baby, you are doing the best you can. And I'm sure you're just fine."

"They're talking about firing me!" As Sean yelled, the red spot on his forehead became darker. It appeared to take on a life of its own and flare up every time Sean yelled out another word. "Everything I do is just wrong. I'm too loud, then I'm too quiet. I'm too gay, then I'm not gay enough. Shit! I never know what they fucking want!" He looked away from Paul. Tears streamed down his face, but he was quiet. Sean sat on the floor, in the corner of their three-bedroom apartment, with his knees up in front of him. He rested his forearms on his knees. Paul knew he'd never be able to say anything that would ever comfort Sean, but he had to say something.

"Well, what are they telling you? What direction are they giving you?"

"They tell me I suck. They stop everything. Make everyone on the set be quiet. And then they tell me I suck, and I should go back to community theatre because I was lucky to find work in Houston to begin with!"

"That just sounds abusive."

"Ya think?"

"But you get through your scenes, right?"

"Yeah, but then they look at the rushes and playbacks and tell me I suck."

"Sean," Paul stopped and waited to see if he'd turn his head. But he didn't. "Are they really saying these things to you? Or are you just feeling…I don't know…insecure about your work?"

"Paul…" Sean closed his eyes and leaned his head back against the wall. "I know what they think about me and it's just…ah fuck. You don't understand. You'll never understand. You've never done anything like this. This is not like the theater shit you did in college. This is a big-time movie. They've got money invested in me, and they're not getting what they want."

"But are they really saying those things to you?"

"Paul, stop! Just leave me alone." Sean stood up and stepped around Paul. "Just take care of the kids and let me get through this."

As Paul leans forward in the clear plastic red chair, his eyes drop away from the Cézanne, and he stares down at the wooden floor.

"Nice floor," he says to no one.

"You okay there, Paul?" Sean walks over and stands between him and the Cézanne.

"Yeah." Paul exhales loudly. "I've just never noticed the floor before." He stands up and walks around Sean. "I generally come here to visit this." He points forward and moves closer to the painting.

"Oh, nice. What's this?" Sean asks. "Cézanne," he continues, blinking his eyes as he focuses on the small sign next to the painting. "Yeah, his work is amazing. And they've got quite a few of his paintings on this floor. There's another portrait of a man over there. Beautiful."

"Yeah. Gustave Geffroy, in the next room. Nice, huh?" Paul turns his head and stares at the face of the man inside the painting. "But this one's pretty unique. Well, at least in this gallery. Even here in Paris."

Sean turns, steps around Paul, and stares up and down at the painting.

"He reminds me of home," Paul continues. "He just doesn't look Parisian or French. Maybe Spanish. Maybe even Mexican." He laughs.

"He actually looks like your tata. Or as I'd always call him, Señor Quintanilla," Sean says, remaining motionless as his eyes move over the canvas and examine every detail of the work.

"Yeah, he really does."

"Must be nice to see someone in one of these paintings who looks like you. Well, I mean, who looks like your tata."

"It is."

They stand together in silence.

"We should really go." Sean steps back, away from the painting. "The kids should be ready to leave, and the car will pick us up at two o'clock."

"Ya know," Paul starts again with a heavier exhale than he had intended. "My tata survived the Mexican Revolution." His eyes fixate on the face of the man inside the painting. "He ran away from General Victoriano Huerta, then Pancho Villa and his men, and then walked from Durango, Mexico, to El Paso, Texas." Paul steps forward, closer to the painting than he had ever stood before. "He'd tell me stories about the dead women he saw all lined up along the roads. And dead men hanging from the trees with ropes around their necks. And the dead animals they'd throw into the rivers and the wells to poison the water."

"Paul," Sean says.

"He was a survivor." Paul steps back.

"I know."

Paul laughs. "We are just complainers. That's all we do. Complain." He steps back even more. "We…we can't even make it through three months of living in a three-bedroom apartment in the beautiful Montparnasse area of Paris without yelling, fighting, and falling apart. All in front of our children."

"I know," Sean says again. "I'm sorry. I really am."

"What if we were to focus on surviving?" Paul turns toward Sean. His face is stern and his voice is steady. "Not just for us, but for our family."

"Yes…okay. I know, you're right."

As dozens of people walk around them to view the Cézanne, they stand together.

"We should go," Paul says, shifting his gaze and shaking his head.

"Okay. But how about we check the gift shop downstairs before we go. Maybe they have a postcard or refrigerator magnet of the Cézanne."

"Okay," Paul says with a laugh.

"It'll just be a reminder of our time here in Paris, and all we've been through."

As they both turn and make their way toward the elevator, Paul feels Sean's arm around his shoulders. Sean smiles, drops his arms down in front of him, and holds his hands out, making a small box-like shape with his fingers. "We'll take a small magnet or postcard of him home." Sean leans back into Paul again and places his arm around him.

"Ugh," Sean complains loudly. "I can't wait to be home."

"Yeah, me too," Paul says, smiling at the thought of a small Cézanne amidst their sons' other drawings, in the middle of their black refrigerator in their four-bedroom home back in Houston.

Rain Dance

Wayne stopped his car in front of the red brick house and expected to see Lynn waiting for him at the front window. He put the car into park, leaned over the passenger's seat, and stared into the large window that faced the front yard. All he could see was the tan blanket Lynn used to cover the back of the couch and the top of the television set.

Wayne parked the car on the street with the two side wheels resting on top of the curb. When he got out of the car, he stood at the end of the driveway. The hedge had grown tall within the past six years. He remembered planting the eight or nine shrubs and watering them religiously month after month in the hopes that one day they would grow together and thicken into a perfectly shaped hedge. He smiled at how crooked the top of the hedge looked and shook his head at how he'd insisted on taking the hedge clippers with him when he moved out. Of all the possessions he'd taken with him during the divorce, Wayne had taken the hedge clippers simply to piss Lynn off.

But she never put up a fight when it came time for him to leave. He remembered her standing at the front window that day with a blank expression. They had not said a word to each other, and she just stood in the middle of the living room waiting patiently for him to leave. He said goodbye as he walked out, but she never replied. She just watched him drive away.

Black rain clouds moved closer to the house from the Tucson Mountains in the west side of town. The sky over the center of town was split right down the center, with the west side of Tucson covered in darkness, and blue sky directly overhead, stretching out farther east. The lighter portion of the sky contained only sparse white clouds that grouped together to form several long lines. The clouds looked alive as they crawled slowly toward the Rincon Mountains on the east side. Wayne was glad he had beaten the rain. The storm would pass by the time he went home that evening.

Wayne rang the doorbell and stepped back in front of the living room window to show Lynn he was at the door. She walked out of the kitchen, glanced up at him, and then walked toward the door, staring down at the floor. When she opened the door, she stepped aside as if she was inviting him in. Wayne smiled at her silent greeting and walked up the step into the house.

As Wayne stood at the front of the living room, he glanced up and turned his head from side to side looking at all the cream-colored splotches that covered the white ceiling. He felt a twinge of pain in his back as he remembered the hours he'd spent painting the ceiling white. The pain intensified as he remembered coming home from work the next day and found Lynn covering the many spots he had missed on the ceiling with the cream-colored paint that was only to be used on the walls. The ceiling still looked like a dove covered with age spots, but the darkening storm would soon hide their mistakes and give him the illusion that they had originally painted the ceiling correctly.

"Please don't mention the goddamn ceiling," Lynn said, standing behind him with her arms crossed.

"It's not my ceiling anymore." Wayne turned his head toward her, raised his eyebrows, and smiled. "So, Lynn, how are you?"

"I'm just great." She walked around him and held her hand out toward the couch in front of the window. "Have a seat and I'll tell you all about it." Lynn sat in the love seat next to the larger couch. Once Lynn had crossed her legs and leaned back in her seat, Wayne walked around the coffee table and sat down. He spread his legs slightly and was about to remove his black baseball cap, when he noticed Lynn watching his every move. He adjusted the brim of his cap and placed it firmly back down on his head.

"It's okay," Lynn said, folding her hands in front of her. She picked up a half-smoked cigarette from the ashtray that rested on the arm of the love seat and lit it with one of the many red lighters scattered throughout the house. Lynn closed her eyes while taking in her first drag. Wayne watched to see if a calmer, less agitated Lynn would look back at him. But she coughed loudly and frantically fanned her right hand in front of her face. She tried desperately to push the smoke behind her and away from Wayne.

"Shit," Lynn said in between coughs. "I'm sorry. I know I probably shouldn't smoke in front of you." When she had successfully cleared most of the air, she leaned over toward the ashtray and crushed out her cigarette.

"It's okay." Wayne leaned forward and placed his elbows on his knees. "I don't think your smoking's gonna hurt me."

"Fuck, Wayne. I'm so sorry. I just wasn't thinking. When you come over, I get so stressed out…that I can't…"

"I know." Wayne stared at the carpet. "Look, Lynn, I'm a little stressed out, too. How 'bout we have ourselves a little drink?"

"Yeah." Lynn smiled at him as she shook her head. "I still

got that bottle of scotch you gave me last New Year's. Want a little Walker and water?"

"I'll take the Walker, but hold the water. I'll get the glasses."

Lynn hopped up from the couch, and he smiled at her as she went to the liquor cabinet. When she bent down and reached inside the open door, Wayne walked into the kitchen and opened the cabinet where they always kept the glasses. He grabbed two and took them to the kitchen table. He put them down on the glass tabletop and leaned forward to look out the window that faced the backyard.

He tried to catch a glimpse of the sky to see if the storm had moved any closer to the house, but all he saw was the roof of the back porch. Two of the grapefruit trees were heavy with light green fruit. In a month or two, the fruit would be ready for picking, and he longed for the taste of fresh-squeezed grapefruit juice with a heavy shot of vodka or tequila.

"This bottle hasn't even been opened yet." Lynn placed the scotch down on the table in front of the glasses.

"That's only because I don't live here anymore." Wayne picked up the bottle and stared down at its label.

"I'd like to say I hate drinking alone," Lynn pulled out one of the chairs and sat down at the table, "but I've really gotten over that since you left. Every Friday night you can find me here drinking a vodka or two, watching the damn grass grow."

Wayne looked out the window and stared at the dead grass that covered most of the yard. He sat down at the table and opened the bottle of scotch. He poured each glass about half full and pushed one over in front of her. She smiled up at him for a second, picked up the glass, and drank the scotch in one swig.

"Please, sir, may I have another?" Lynn laughed as she closed her eyes. She shifted her head from side to side and exhaled. Wayne gulped his scotch down and poured two more. This time his pouring was a little heavier, and he held on to the bottle just in case Lynn slammed her second glass. Lynn leaned her head forward as she took a small sip.

"So, how's your fucking job?" Lynn rested her elbows on the table with the glass of scotch still in her right hand.

"Work's the same." Wayne took his own sip and leaned back in the chair. "I'm only there about two days a week, and I'll be taking more time off at the end of the month."

"Really? I talked to Katie last weekend. She sends her best and says she'll talk with you when she comes home for a visit in a few weeks."

"How's her school going?" Wayne held his glass with both hands as it rested on the table in front of him.

"Good. She says she has a graduate assistantship for next semester, and she's planning on graduating next May. I told her I didn't know if you would be able to make it to graduation, but I would drive the both of us up there if you could."

"That'd be nice." Wayne raised his glass once again. "We'll just have to see what I feel like next May."

"I know," Lynn replied. "And Katie knows that, too. I guess we're just hoping for the best."

"That's fine, Lynn, you don't have to explain." Wayne could hear the sound of thunder as the storm drew closer.

"It's getting hot in here," Lynn said, as she stared down at her empty glass. She leaned farther back in the chair, reached down, and pulled the front of her shirt out of her jeans. She tilted her head to one side and widened her eyes. "How 'bout some ice for that scotch?"

"Sounds good." Wayne laughed as she held on to the back of the chair and stood up. She opened the freezer behind him and cracked a tray of ice into the empty bin. With three ice cubes in each hand, she returned to the table and dropped them into their glasses. Without a word, Wayne poured more scotch, and they both sat together quietly, waiting for the storm to move in.

The sound of the hail outside finally broke their silence, and they both leaned closer to the window. The hail bounced off the cement walkway that led to the back gate, and the accumulating hail began to make white patches on top of the hay-colored grass. The hail that accumulated closer to the sprinkler heads throughout the lawn contrasted nicely with the green grass that grew around each one.

Lynn steadied herself again, stood up, and walked over to the box hanging on the wall next to the refrigerator. It had *coffin nails* painted in black across the front. She pulled out a fresh pack and the red lighter she also kept inside the box. When she sat back down at the table, she leaned in closer to Wayne. "I'm sorry, I just can't take it anymore."

Wayne also leaned forward, trying to hear Lynn over the hail that crashed against the tin roof that covered the patio. "It's okay. Don't worry about it."

Lynn lit her cigarette and turned her head to blow the smoke away from Wayne. When the loud hail had turned into a heavy rain, she cleared her throat and held the lit cigarette at the side of her face.

"You always hated it when I smoked, didn't you?" Her tone was much louder than necessary since the crashing hail outside had stopped.

"Because you only smoke when you're nervous or drunk."

"Well, I'm not nervous now." She continued to laugh and rubbed the side of her face with the hand that wasn't holding her cigarette.

"Remember that night in Vegas, when we won all that money and ordered those expensive cigars?" Wayne laughed to himself as he filled his glass with more scotch and crossed his legs.

"And that fucking dealer made some crack at me when I lit my cigar like, 'Oh, that's real ladylike.'" Lynn's speech was beginning to slur. "Those days we drank tequila. Eh!" She wrinkled her nose, and a look of disgust covered her face.

"Yeah, but then we moved on to whiskey." Wayne also made a face, closed his eyes, and shook his head.

Lynn stopped laughing and listened to the rain as it continued to pour heavily outside. "But then we got pregnant."

"Yeah," Wayne replied, as he remembered the time during her pregnancy when they actually stopped drinking. After Katie was born, they'd stay home, put her to sleep in the nursery, and go outside to drink on the patio. The cycle had begun once again, and they quickly moved from beer and wine to tequila and whiskey. And when Katie could finally sleep through the night, they switched to scotch and would sit together for hours staring at the moon.

Wayne stared up at the ceiling. The rain was still heavy, but the silence between claps of thunder was growing longer and longer. He looked back down at the scotch. The red and gold label on the bottle glowed as if it had a light of its own.

"Do you want me to turn on the light?" Lynn said.

"No, it's not that dark."

"Okay," she said. She picked up the bottle once again and poured herself another glass. Wayne smiled at the sight of his ex-wife with a cigarette hanging from the side of her mouth and the bottle of scotch covering part of her face.

"What?" she asked as she placed the bottle back down on the table.

"Nothing," Wayne said, and his smile turned into laughter.

"Fucker," Lynn mumbled as she dragged on her cigarette.

After another long stretch of silence, Lynn drank some more scotch and crushed her cigarette out in the ashtray she kept on the window sill. She held the glass of scotch up in front of her face, closed one eye, and peered at Wayne through the dark liquid. She laughed for a second but then held the glass in front of her mouth and stared at him.

"You know," she began, trying to sit up straight and banging her scotch down on the glass tabletop. "I really hated you when I was alone." She leaned her head forward and smacked her lips. "After you moved out, and Katie went away to college."

"I know." Wayne held his own glass up to his mouth but stopped before taking another drink.

"After that, I was always alone." Lynn let go of the glass. "The one thing I thought I wanted most in the world was driving me crazy." She pressed her lips tightly together. "And I thought I hated you because you left me alone. I know..." Lynn stopped and sat perfectly still. "I know you wanted to be with a man, not me, and you had to come out of the closet and find yourself. But I really hated you for leaving me alone." She cleared her throat. "Alone at my age."

"I'd changed, Lynn." She pulled her feet up on the chair and hugged her knees. "I wanted something different. And I didn't want to be married to you anymore."

"We both wanted that."

"It's funny." Wayne held her gaze and leaned his head back. "It's only when we both want something that we end up getting it."

"And we both wanted a divorce."

"Yeah."

Wayne continued to watch the rain as it washed away the white patches of hail and replaced them with shallow pools of dark water. When the rain had lightened, and the thunder could no longer be heard, Lynn said, "I'm still hot. You wanna go out and sit on the patio?"

As Wayne walked outside, he noticed Lynn had painted the roof of the patio and had actually gone out and bought some new deck chairs. When he asked her about it, she replied, "Yeah, I found a lot of furniture on sale now that it's monsoon season. I guess people don't sit outside like us after the rains."

They sat down together in two new chairs that stood at the edge of the patio. Wayne had carried the bottle of scotch outside even though Lynn's glass was still about half full. He leaned over to one side and placed the bottle underneath his chair. He noticed her hair was longer. With her head still facing forward, Lynn turned her eyes toward Wayne. After a while, she began to laugh. Wayne laughed with her, and she looked over at him with embarrassment.

"Would you believe I'm actually cold now?"

Without a word, Wayne reached around and picked up the bottle of scotch.

"I think I actually need a coat," Lynn said, holding up her glass and showing him she still had quite a bit of scotch left. "Did you bring a jacket with you?"

"No."

"I'll see if I can get you a blanket or something."

"That'd be great."

Lynn was gone for only a few minutes, and when she returned, she ran out of the house wearing her green windbreaker and holding one of Wayne's old coats at a distance in front of her.

"Can you believe I still have this old thing?"

Wayne laughed as she draped the short black raincoat down over the front of her body.

"You wore this every day in college. Remember?"

"Yeah." Wayne's head ached with the old memory and the thought of how he was going to turn fifty-three next month.

"College algebra," Lynn said. "I remember how you'd run in late and you'd always be wearing this damn black raincoat."

"Hey, it was the only coat I had." Wayne reached over and touched the coat's sleeve.

"And it rained all the time that semester." Lynn held the coat closer to her body and laughed.

"I came from Ohio, Lynn. Who the fuck knew it rained so much in Tucson?"

"Ohio boy," Lynn teased. She handed him the coat and lowered her head. "You were cute when you were a freshman," she said. "Your hair was always slicked back and wet from the rain."

Wayne lifted his hand and adjusted the brim of his baseball cap. Lynn began to laugh again. By the time she sat back down in her chair, she was doubled over with her head turned in the opposite direction.

At first Wayne smiled at her laughter, but he took another sip of scotch and began to laugh along with her. Lynn's laughter began to take on a much lower sound, and Wayne saw the tears in her eyes. He sat back in his chair and waited for Lynn to take a deep breath. Once her breathing began to take on a regular rhythm, he tilted his head and asked her to look up at him. When Lynn finally sat up straight, she looked directly in front of her and watched the rain with red, tired eyes. She rubbed frantically at the tears on her face, rocking back and forth in her chair as she slowly calmed herself down.

"When Katie told me you were sick, I thought maybe it was my fault," She said. "Like I had driven you crazy, and your poor mind just couldn't take it anymore. And then I thought maybe it was my smoking, and then…" Lynn took another deep breath and held it. "I thought it was all the drinking. But now I just don't know what to think." Lynn held her hand up over her mouth and tears streamed down her face.

"You know me, Lynn. I've never been able to take care of myself." Wayne leaned in closer and waited for her to stop crying.

The colors of the backyard began to brighten once again. A light rain still fell, but the sun was coming out somewhere in front of the house. Lynn pressed her lips together and stood up. She walked out from underneath the patio and stood a short distance in front of Wayne. Beyond the fence, the dark rain clouds continued to move farther east, and darkness now covered most of the Rincon Mountains.

Lynn tilted her head back to feel the rain on her face, and the back of her head suddenly rested on Wayne's chest. He stepped forward and wrapped his arms carefully around her waist. Lynn relaxed her body and leaned in closer to him. After a few minutes of watching the dark clouds move farther and farther away, Wayne dropped his hands and tried to turn Lynn toward him.

"Here," he said. "Why don't you look at the sky that's over in the west?"

Lynn lifted her head and glanced over his shoulder. She smiled and pulled her hands up to her face. She reached up and lifted the back of her hair off her shoulders. "I must look really great, huh?"

"You look fine," he replied as she combed her hands through her hair. "Here," he said, lowering his head and removing his baseball cap. "Take this."

Lynn took the cap from him, tucked her hair up into it, and pulled it down over her head. She smiled as she adjusted the brim in front of her. But her smile disappeared when she saw that the skin at the top of Wayne's forehead was red and cracked. Just above his right ear, she saw a long scar that stretched across the side of his head like a closed zipper surrounded by dry and damaged skin.

"My God." Lynn reached her shaking hand up toward his forehead. "This is from your radiation?"

"Yeah." Wayne lowered his head to bring it closer to Lynn's hand. "After the surgery, I went through a couple weeks of treatment to kill the rest of the cancer, but I had to stop. They just make me too sick, and they don't really help that much anyway. Sure, I might live a little longer, but it's just more time I'll end up spending in hospice." Wayne's voice was calm and low.

Lynn rested her hand at the top of Wayne's head where the skin was still healthy and pale. She moved it slowly toward his right ear and rubbed his scar and the burn marks that were left by the radiation. With her other hand, Lynn pulled Wayne closer to her and held on to the side of his raincoat. She continued to caress the top of his head and then began to press down harder, trying to rub the raindrops into his skin. She then stopped and pulled her hand away as Wayne lifted his head. Still holding him close to her, she placed her hand back over her mouth and began to cry. She cried so hard her body began to tremble, and she lowered her head so the brim of Wayne's baseball cap would cover her face. Wayne pulled her closer to him and rested his chin on the top of her head.

"It's okay," he said. He held on to her with both hands and began to rock with her back and forth. "It's okay."

When Lynn stopped crying, she pressed her head up against Wayne's chest as the rain began to run down the brim of her cap.

Still rocking back and forth, Lynn pulled her head away from Wayne's chest and placed her arms around the back of his neck.

"I did love you at one time, Wayne," she said. "And it's okay that you changed. It's okay that you wanted something different. I'm okay with all of that now."

"I know." Their rocking back and forth turned to swaying side to side. "I wish I could tell you I was going to be okay, but I can't. I just want you to know if I'm healthy enough, I'd like to go to Katie's graduation."

"Okay." Lynn pulled her arms away from his neck, pushed them underneath his raincoat, and wrapped them around his waist. She rested her head up against his chest and said, "I'll take you, Wayne. Please don't worry about that."

"But if I'm really sick, I want you to always remind Katie how proud I am of her. I tell her as often as I can. But please, always remind her." Wayne lowered his eyes and stared at the top of his baseball cap.

"Anything," Lynn whispered. "I'll help you with anything, just let me know."

White clouds now moved directly over the grapefruit trees. The rain had finally stopped, but Lynn continued to hold tightly to Wayne's waist. He looked back over at the bottle of scotch and wished he'd brought his glass out into the rain. He knew it would still be there when they finally went inside, so he pressed his hand up against Lynn's back and continued to sway with her side to side. The dark storm clouds moved farther and farther away, and Wayne smiled at the thought of how much he had come to love the monsoon rains in Tucson.

About the Author

Andrew L. Huerta lives in Tucson, Arizona, where he has spent the last twenty-four years working in higher education. As the instructor and advisor of undergraduate students who are the first in their families to go to college, Andrew teaches technical and professional writing courses that prepare students for their transition into graduate education. As the youngest in a Mexican-American family of six children, much of Andrew's inspiration comes from his Huerta-Lopez family history. The remainder of his stories, both fiction and nonfiction, come from his travels, his time in Education, and his varied life experience in and around southern Arizona.

Books Available From Bold Strokes Books

Busy Ain't the Half of It by Frederick Smith and Chaz Lamar Cruz. Elijah and Justin seek happily-ever-afters in LA, but are they too busy to notice happiness when it's there? (978-1-63555-944-6)

Pursuit: A Victorian Entertainment by Felice Picano. An intelligent, handsome, ruthlessly ambitious young man who rose from the slums to become the right-hand man of the Lord Exchequer of England will stop at nothing as he pursues his Lord's vanished wife across Continental Europe. (978-1-63555-870-8)

Best of the Wrong Reasons by Sander Santiago. For Fin Ness and Orion Starr, it takes a funeral to remind them that love is worth living for. (978-1-63555-867-8)

Coming to Life on South High by Lee Patton. Twenty-one-year-old gay virgin Gabe Rafferty's first adult decade unfolds as an unpredictable journey into sex, love, and livelihood. (978-1-63555-906-4)

Death's Prelude by David S. Pederson. In this prequel to the Detective Heath Barrington Mystery series, Heath discovers that first love changes you forever and drives you to become the person you're destined to be. (978-1-63555-786-2)

His Brother's Viscount by Stephanie Lake. Hector Somerville wants to rekindle his illicit love affair with Viscount Wentworth, but he must overcome one problem: Wentworth still loves Hector's brother. (978-1-63555-805-0)

The Dubious Gift of Dragon Blood by J. Marshall Freeman. One day Crispin is a lonely high school student—the next he is fighting a war in a land ruled by dragons, his otherworldly boyfriend at his side. (978-1-63555-725-1)

Quake City by St John Karp. Can Andre find his best friend Amy before the night devolves into a nightmare of broken hearts, malevolent drag queens, and spontaneous human combustion? Or has it always happened this way, every night, at Aunty Bob's Quake City Club? (978-1-63555-723-7)

Death Overdue by David S. Pederson. Did Heath turn to murder in an alcohol-induced haze to solve the problem of his blackmailer, or was it someone else who brought about a death overdue? (978-1-63555-711-4)

Every Summer Day by Lee Patton. Meant to celebrate every summer day, Luke's journal instead chronicles a love affair as fast-moving and possibly as fatal as his brother's brain tumor. (978-1-63555-706-0)

Everyday People by Louis Barr. When film star Diana Danning hires private eye Clint Steele to find her son, Clint turns to his former West Point barracks mate, and ex-buddy with benefits, Mars Hauser to lend his cyber espionage and digital black ops skills to the case.(978-1-63555-698-8)

Cirque des Freaks and Other Tales of Horror by Julian Lopez. Explore the pleasure of horror in this compilation that delivers like the horror classics…good ole tales of terror. (978-1-63555-689-6)

Royal Street Reveillon by Greg Herren. In this Scotty Bradley mystery, someone is killing the stars of a reality show, and it's up to Scotty Bradley and the boys to find out who. (978-1-63555-545-5)

Death Takes a Bow by David S. Pederson. Alan Keys takes part in a local stage production, but when the leading man is murdered, his partner Detective Heath Barrington is thrust into the limelight to find the killer. (978-1-63555-472-4)

Accidental Prophet by Bud Gundy. Days after his grandmother dies, Drew Morten learns his true identity and finds himself racing against time to save civilization from the apocalypse. (978-1-63555-452-6)

Counting for Thunder by Phillip Irwin Cooper. A struggling actor returns to the Deep South to manage a family crisis but finds love and ultimately his own voice as his mother is regaining hers for possibly the last time. (978-1-63555-450-2)

Of Echoes Born by 'Nathan Burgoine. A collection of queer fantasy short stories set in Canada from Lambda Literary Award finalist 'Nathan Burgoine. (978-1-63555-096-2)

www.ingramcontent.com/pod-product-compliance
Lightning Source LLC
Chambersburg PA
CBHW032149020726
47496CB00003B/785